Bourbon and Burlesque

LOVE AND LIBATIONS BOOK THREE

RAQUEL RILEY

Copyright © 2023 by Raquel Riley

www.raquelriley.com

All rights reserved.

No part of this book may be used, reproduced, or transmitted in any form or by any electronic or mechanical means, including information storage and retrieval systems, without written permission from the author, except for the use of brief quotations in a book review.

This is a work of fiction. Names, characters, places, and incidents either are the product of the author's imagination or are used fictitiously. Any resemblance to actual persons, living or dead, businesses, companies, events, or locales is entirely coincidental. The use of any real company and/or product names is for literary effect only. All products and brand names are registered trademarks of their respective holders/companies.

This book contains sexually explicit material which is only suitable for mature audiences.

Edited by Elli at Clocktower Editing

Cover design by Raquel Riley

Proofreading by Mildred Jordan

For Kelley,
*You danced into my head wearing a bright smile
and red heels and stole my heart.
Throughout the duration of telling your story,
you kept me laughing.*

For Graham,
*You needed sunshine and laughter in your life,
and I found the perfect man to shine
a bright light into all of your dark shadows.
Thank you for doing such an amazing job
looking after all of my boys.*

Carrick Family Tree

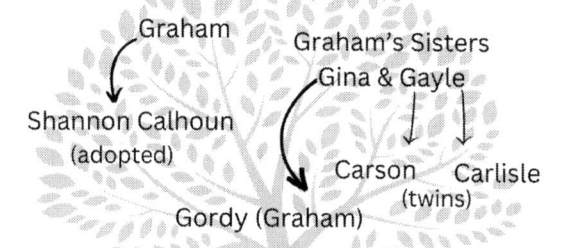

Graham
↳ Shannon Calhoun (adopted)

Graham's Sisters
Gina & Gayle
↓   ↓
Carson   Carlisle
(twins)

Gordy (Graham)

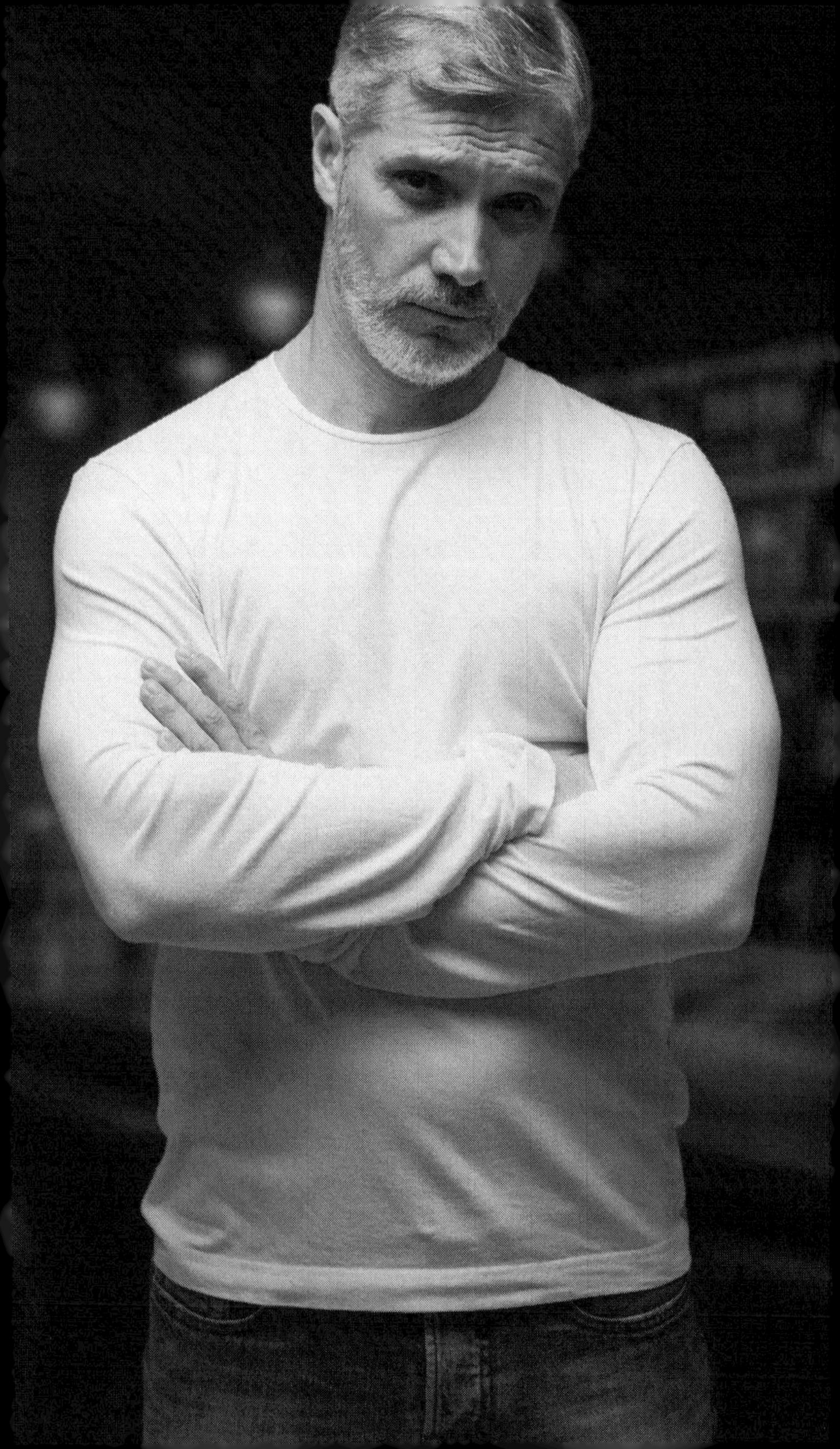

> He was enough temptation for twenty men, and I was only one man.
>
> —Graham Carrick

Bourbon AND Burlesque

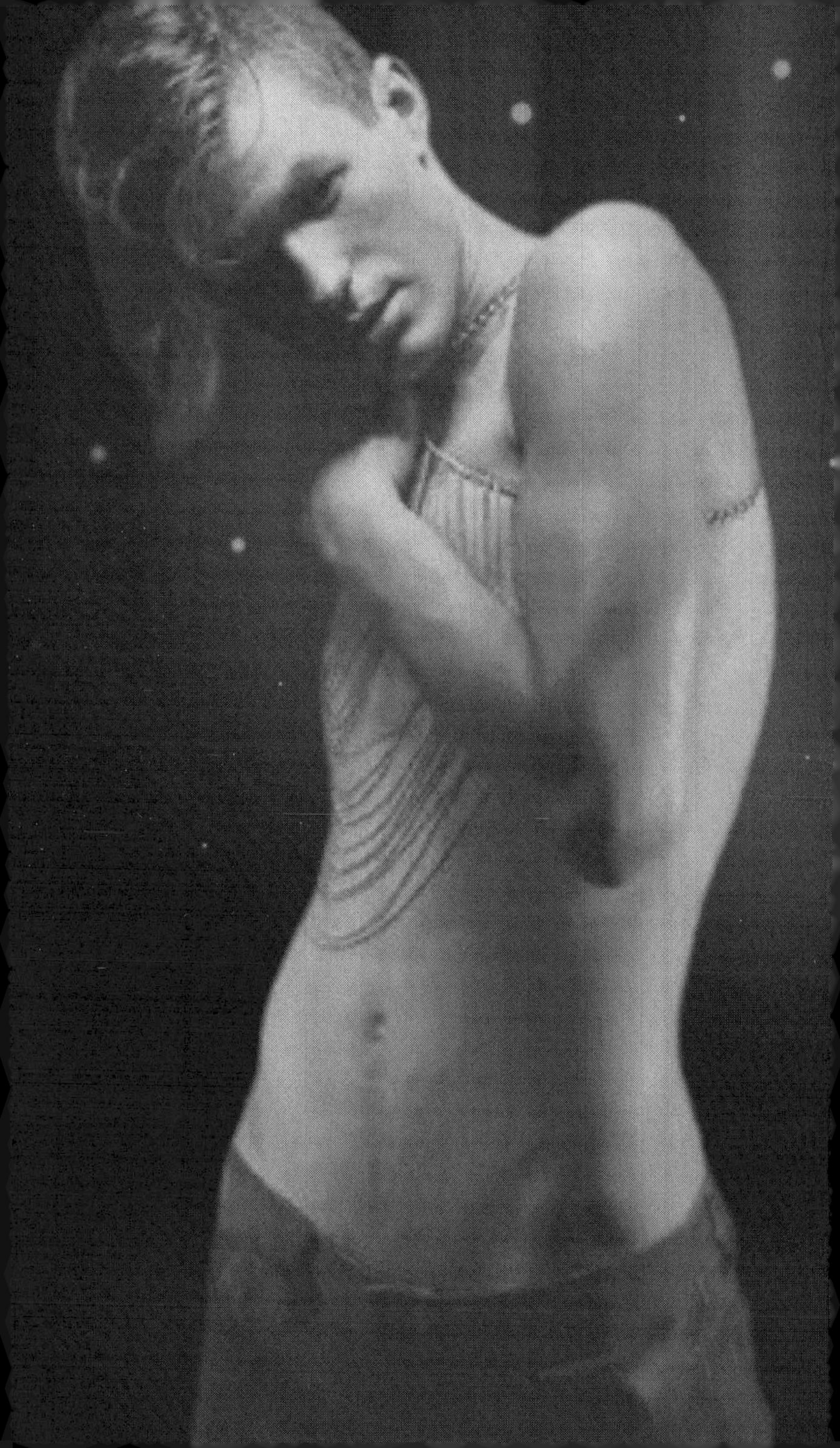

I wanted him to want me. Maybe because I respected him so much. If a man that I admired was attracted to me, did that make me a better person?

—Kelley Michaelson

Bourbon AND Burlesque

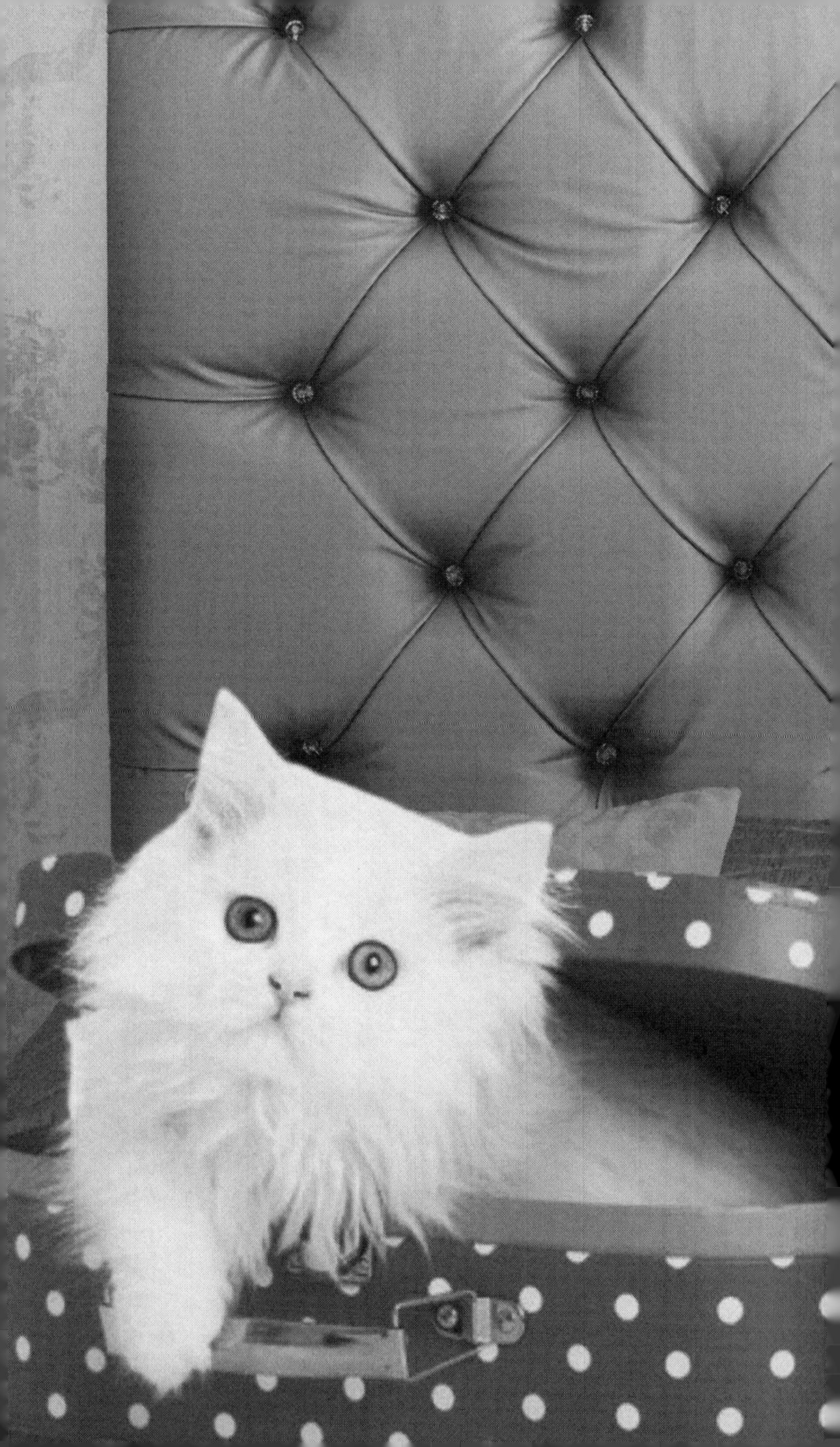

My name is Glitter because I shone the brightest in the litter.

—Glitter

Bourbon and Burlesque

CONTENT WARNING

This book contains stalking with escalated violence. Also mention of alcohol consumption.

1

GRAHAM

I FUCKING HATED HOSPITALS. Usually, nothing good happened there. In fact, the only thing I might hate more was being stuck in traffic when I was in a goddamn hurry. The guy in front of me going twenty miles too slowly picked the wrong day to get in my way. Because not only was I stuck in traffic, I was on my way to the hospital. Twenty minutes ago, my nephew called to tell me my best friend had been stabbed in front of my bar. A sick feeling had settled into the pit of my belly, like acid, burning a hole through the lining of my stomach.

I punched the horn in the center of my steering wheel, the blaring sound making several drivers turn to look at me, and the guy in front of me flipped me off. *Yeah, you, too, buddy.* I pulled around him and stepped on the gas, passing three cars, swung a sharp left turn, cutting off another driver, and pulled into the parking lot of the hospital, practically splitting my forehead open on the steering wheel when I took a speed bump too fast.

The parking lot was full, so I pulled into the first

open space closest to the ER, which belonged to a Dr. C. Richards, whoever that was, and hauled ass inside.

"Whoa, Pops. Wait up!"

I stopped dead in my tracks and turned around. "Shannon, thank God. How is he?"

My son wrapped me in a bear hug. "He's good."

I pulled back to stare into his eyes, trying to read what he meant by 'good'.

"Don't bullshit me, Shannon."

"I swear, Pops, he's good. They're stitching him up right now. But his x-rays were clean. No damage to his internal organs. As soon as they finish patching him up, they're gonna move him into a private room. Then we can go visit."

I exhaled a deep breath and scrubbed my face. "Thank God." My nephew, Carson, walked over. He ended his phone call and slipped the phone into his back pocket.

"Hey, Uncle G. Good to see you. Rory's gonna be fine."

"I'm glad to hear it. Why doesn't somebody tell me what the fuck happened?"

"It all started with that dancer, Kelley Michaelson."

"The little blond who does the burlesque routine?" I questioned.

"He's not so little." Carson snickered before Shannon elbowed him, frowning.

Shannon continued. "Yeah. He apparently has a stalker. Rory noticed something was off with a customer during Kelley's performance and decided to keep his eye on him. When he walked Kelley out to his car at the end of the night, I guess the guy got jealous, thinking Rory was taking Kelley home with him. The guy tried to run them down, but Rory dodged the car. Then he got out and just stabbed him, right here," he said, pointing at his side.

"Christ! Did they catch him?"

"Not yet," Carson said. "He took off."

"Where's Kelley? Is he hurt?"

"He's all right. A little banged up, but he'll be fine. He's giving his statement to the police right now."

"Un-fucking-believable. What makes people do the things they do?" I crossed my arms over my chest and exhaled another deep breath, trying to get a hold of my emotions. My temper was quickly running away from me. I followed Shannon and Carson to the waiting room at the end of the hall. It was packed with people, but I spied Ryan, Carson's boyfriend, and my nephew Gordy seated in the corner. "Where's Carlisle?"

"He's in with Rory," Carson answered.

Figures. I wouldn't expect him to be anywhere else. My nephew was falling hard and fast, well, maybe not so fast, for my best friend. It was a situation I was still trying to wrap my head around.

Kelley wandered in, shuffling one foot in front of the other too slowly, like he had no destination in mind. He looked completely unrecognizable from the last time I saw him, standing up on stage under the spotlights, moving his body sinuously to the music as he twisted and turned in ways I hadn't known were possible. This version of Kelley was smeared with dirt, road-rash scratches covered his arms, and his eyes were red. Streaks of black mascara ran down his cheeks, and his hair was a mess. Yet, somehow, he was still a beautiful man.

I waved him over, and he came, slowly, but willingly, and joined our group. Ryan stood, offering Kelley his seat. He gave Kelley a hug, and Kelley melted into him, accepting his comfort. Ryan was one of those men who gave affection easily. The rest of my boys, not so much. Myself included. I listened as Kelley recounted his story, going over the details he gave in his statement. He seemed to be blaming himself for my best friend's injury, which wouldn't do at all. It wasn't his responsibility to carry the burden of other people's actions. I'd known Rory for more than twenty years. He was always going to play the hero. It was a trait of his personality that ran bone-deep. Protecting people and saving lives came as naturally to him as breathing. That was why I hired him to watch over my family in my absence as I ran another bar across town. I trusted him with my life and with the lives of my boys. And I knew without a doubt that he would have risked his life to save Kelley's. It wasn't something Kelley should feel at fault for.

Shannon spoke up. "Listen, they're probably gonna call us back there soon. Why don't we head into the gift shop and see if we can find something to cheer him up? We can't show up empty-handed." My son was something else. Smooth, diplomatic, and a natural born leader. I knew he was trying to distract everyone and keep their spirits up.

The crew shifted toward the gift shop, and I followed behind next to Shannon. "You and I both know there's not a damn thing in that store he wants that would cheer him up."

Shannon nodded. "Pretty sure all he wants are some painkillers and Carlisle." He laughed at my dark scowl.

That SOB was damn lucky to have landed my nephew. Considering the seventeen-year age gap between them, despite the fact that my nephew was a grown man, he was lucky I didn't cut his balls off.

I addressed my boys wandering aimlessly around the store in a state of confusion. "His favorite color is pink," I falsely informed them. Shannon laughed, shaking his head.

We headed to the third floor waiting room with our arms full of pink flowers, cards, balloons, and stuffed plushies. This room was much smaller than the waiting room downstairs in the general lobby, and our group took up most of it. Shannon poured himself a cup of coffee while we waited, and it wasn't long before a nurse popped her head in to inform us he was ready for visitors.

We quietly filed into his tiny room, and of course, the first thing I saw was my nephew Carlisle cozying up in bed with my best friend, tucked right into Rory's side. Rory's satisfied smile put me at ease because I knew he was going to be all right if his greatest priority was trying to piss me off. I glanced at his monitors, trying to make sense of the numbers. I didn't know what it all meant, but nothing was blinking red, and there were no alarms going off, so I took that as a good sign. Rory checked in with each one of my boys, trying to convince them he was going to be fine, and then his nurse shuffled back in to tell us visiting hours were winding down. Carlisle put up a fierce stance about why he believed he should stay the night with Rory until he was discharged.

"I'll be back to get you in the morning," Shannon informed him with a pointed look.

Rory winked at him. "Hopefully not too early."

As we were leaving, Rory said, "Kelley, hold up a minute. Can I have a word with you?"

I could guess what he wanted to talk about. Kelley looked torn up with guilt. Seeing Rory bruised and bandaged, surrounded by tubes and beeping machines, didn't help. Carlisle and I went out into the hall to give them privacy, but I left the door cracked behind me, eavesdropping on their conversation. Although my boys would never admit it, they still looked up to me as the head of our family. I felt it was my responsibility to make everything run smoothly for everyone. And though Kelley wasn't one of my boys, it made no difference. I hadn't seen any of his family show up to comfort him. He seemed to be all alone in the world, and I had a habit of collecting lost boys, gathering them into my herd like stray sheep. I was going to keep an eye on him until they caught his attacker. Someone needed to keep him safe, and I hadn't seen anyone stepping up to volunteer besides me.

Their voices drifted through the crack in the door.

"But until they catch him, I don't want you to stay alone. Don't go anywhere on your own. Do you have somewhere safe where you can stay?"

"I don't need to be a burden to anyone. I'll be fine."

That was code for 'I have no one to rely on, and nowhere else to go'. He was wrong. One hundred percent incorrect. Whether or not he realized it, he had me. I wouldn't fail him.

Stepping back into the room, I met Rory's gaze over Kelley's shoulder. "Don't worry, he has a safe place to stay. I'll make sure he goes nowhere alone."

Predictably, Kelley blanched, before turning beet red. I ushered him out of the room.

"If you've wrapped up all your loose ends, I'll drive you home so you can get some rest."

"H-home? To my place?" he asked, his hand fluttering to his chest.

"No, to my place. You're coming home with me so I can keep an eye on you. You ready?"

IT SEEMED like with every passing birthday, I became less human in the mornings. Which was why the bar business suited me just fine. It catered to the night owls, like me. I filled my mug with straight espresso, not a hint of cream or milk in sight, grabbed my newspaper, and headed into the living room.

The sight that greeted me made me fumble my mug, spilling hot coffee over my bare chest and burning my damn nipples.

"Fuck, that's hot!"

Kelley's head whipped around, eyes wide.

He was bent over with his perfect bubble ass high in the air. The stretchy white leggings he wore showed every curve and dip in his voluptuous body. The red thong he wore beneath glowed bright like a neon sign.

"I meant the coffee!" Shit, could I sound any more perverted?

"I'm so sorry, let me help you," he offered, rushing over to take my mug and the paper from me.

He smelled like a tropical beach, coconut and sugar, and his nails were painted bright red to match his thong. A bead of sweat rolled down his throat and dropped between his toned pecs, adding to the moisture soaking into his white cotton cropped tank. The sweat made it almost sheer, his dark pink nipples peeking through. Like a horny teenager, my gaze was solidly fixed on his pumped chest. I swiped the wet drips of coffee from my skin, dried my hand on my shorts, and reached for my mug and paper.

"Am I in your way?"

"No! No, go ahead and continue. I'm just going to sit over here and read the paper." I sat down on the couch and unfolded the newspaper. Kelley looked skeptical but resumed his yoga. My eyes continued to follow him over the edge of my paper as he bent and stretched, his long, toned limbs undulating beneath the thin Lycra. I read the same article three times before I gave up and stared unabashedly at Kelley.

"I feel like you're watching me. Am I distracting you?"

I rustled the paper to make it sound as if I were turning pages. "Not at all. You're fine. Sorry if I broke your concentration."

Kelley moved into an obscene position, his body completely bent in half as he peeked at me from between his legs. "You know, you should try this. It increases your flexibility, strengthens your joints, and improves your circulation and blood flow as well."

I chuffed a short breath through my nose. There was nothing wrong with my blood flow, except for the fact that it was all centered in one part of my body at the moment. I crossed one leg over the other at the knee to hide my growing erection.

"I'm afraid I would slip a disk or throw a hip out."

Kelley unfolded his body, arching into a bridge that showed off the beautiful curve of his spine. "Nonsense," he exclaimed. "It opens your chakras and increases your energy, strengthens your core. I promise you'll feel ten years younger."

He collapsed from his position, landing in a graceful heap on his purple mat. "I mean, *feel*, like I said, not look. There's nothing wrong with the way you look," he said, blushing.

Christ, I thought. What the fuck am I doing panting after a guy who is younger than my son? A guy who just reminded me we were born in different decades. Hell, probably different centuries.

A drop of sweat slid down the valley of his carved stomach, pooling in his bellybutton. My throat was parched, but not for coffee. I wanted to lick the sweat from his body.

"If you change your mind, let me know. I would love to help you stretch. I could even help you hold your position until you can manage it on your own."

The thought of his hands on my body, stretching my muscles taut, had me leaking in my shorts.

"Yeah? Let me think about it. So after yoga, what did you have planned today?"

"A hot shower."

Interesting, I would be taking a cold one.

"Breakfast, and then," he shrugged.

"Kelley, you are not a prisoner here. You can come and go as you please. I'll just be coming with you."

He had been here for the last two days and had not once asked to leave, wearing the spare clothes he had in his duffel bag the night of the accident.

"But you have a lot on your plate. You are the head of your family, and you have two bars to run. You have your own life. You've done enough for me."

I laid the newspaper down, giving him my full attention. "Thank you for making me sound like I lead a more interesting life than I really do. Shannon and Carlisle cover all of my bookkeeping and supply shipments. They run the bars seamlessly. They don't need me. My boys are all grown now and have lives of their own. If there's something you need to do today, I'm all yours."

"Well," he smiled shyly. "There is one place I've been dying to go."

2

KELLEY

"REALLY? THIS WAS YOUR LONG-NEGLECTED ERRAND?"

Graham looked completely out of place, surrounded by fluffy, mewling kittens, a stark contrast to his dark tattoos and black leather boots. It was hard to maintain the grumpy and gruff bad boy biker image while holding a precious little calico baby. Another kitten, a tiny gray Himalayan with more fluff than actual body weight, clawed its way up his T-shirt.

"These are my babies! My fur babies." I stroked the tabby in my arms. "I'm not allowed to have pets, according to my lease. But it's just impossible to hold a puppy or a kitten and have a negative thought. Everything just melts away when I come here and hold them. It's my happy place."

"So, what do you do here?"

"Just play with them. Sometimes, I feed them treats from my hand. The puppies like to go outside in the courtyard and run around. I take pictures of them and post them on the shelter's website in hopes they'll get adopted quicker."

A mixed orange kitten crawled into my lap, and I stroked between his ears, smiling when he began to purr like a motorboat.

"So, is photography a thing you do, like a hobby or something?"

"Oh, no. Not at all. I just take pictures with my phone. They don't turn out great or anything, but something is better than nothing. Who could resist a cute little kitten wearing a bow tie?"

I gave him a sunny smile, and he returned it, until the kitten on his shirt began to scratch at his salt and pepper beard. He flinched when the razor-sharp nails sank into his chin. I'd become used to the feeling, but I knew how much it hurt. It felt like little razor blades slicing your skin. Like a thousand tiny paper cuts.

Graham gently disentangled the kitten and placed it on the floor by his feet.

"Besides spending your days off playing the Pied Piper with all of these babies, what else do you do with your time? I can't imagine dancing on Friday nights at the bar is your only job."

"Not by a long shot," I answered, laughing at the idea that I spent all week petting kittens and puppies. "I teach dance and burlesque at the studio downtown. I'm also a yoga instructor at a day spa. And when I work out at the gym, I record it with my phone and upload the videos to my social media accounts. Like a guided training session."

"Really? Social media, huh? Do you have a lot of

followers? I mean, I can't imagine people wouldn't want to watch you work out."

I could've sworn he was flushed, but he looked down at his feet, rubbing the back of his neck, and I couldn't see his face clearly.

"I'm getting there. The account is growing by leaps and bounds every month. It really blows me away. In addition to the guided workouts, I upload meditation videos, nutrition and supplement shake combinations, and healthy meal prep ideas."

"Wow, you make me sound lazy. Is there anything you don't do online?"

He smiled, and I'm sure he meant it as a compliment because he sounded mildly impressed, but then his eyes widened horrifically, and I definitely saw him blush, without a doubt. Graham slapped his hand over his mouth.

"Oh, my God, I did not mean that like it sounded. I mean, not that there's anything wrong with that, if that's what you do. I would certainly pay—" He shook his head frantically. "No, I mean, not me *personally*, because I *would*, but I'm not—"

His words cut off abruptly, and he hid his face in his hands. His shoulders began to shake uncontrollably, and I realized he was silently laughing at himself. He had to feel completely embarrassed. I set the kittens down and crawled to him on my knees, gently tugging his hands from his face. I only wanted to put him at ease after the incredible generosity and kindness he'd shown me.

"I know what you meant," I assured him. "And I'm flattered that you would pay to watch me."

His head snapped up, and I couldn't contain my smile as it stretched across my entire face. It must have been contagious because Graham smiled as well. We both fell into a fit of laughter, surrounded by a rag-tag army of floofy kittens scratching at our pants.

I was finally able to catch my breath, sinking to my bottom on the floor as Graham sat up straight and breathed a deep breath, his broad chest expanding as his T-shirt stretched even tighter.

He sighed loudly. "God, it feels good to laugh like that. I can't remember the last time I did." He gazed at me, eyes shining, and I noticed for the first time just how deep of a green his irises were. Like the color of shamrocks. Kelly Green, like my name. "I bet you're not a day over twenty-four."

Smiling, I answered, "I'll be twenty-five soon."

Graham shook his head and smiled.

"What?" I asked as I giggled self-consciously.

"You have a distinct way of making me feel very old and yet somehow young again and full of life at the same time."

My heart danced a tango in my chest. "I don't know whether you mean that as a compliment or not."

"Neither do I." He laughed. "Do you need to run by the studio? Or the spa?"

"No, I don't have any classes scheduled today."

"Perfect, then I can take you to lunch after this."

WE SETTLED ON A SUSHI RESTAURANT, and I had a feeling he had agreed because it seemed to make me happy. I doubted Graham knew anything about sushi. My suspicions were confirmed when he asked me to order for him, and then puzzled over how to hold his chopsticks. I leaned across the table, putting my hand over his, as I corrected the position of his fingers on the wooden sticks. My navy and white polka dot blouse gaped open, providing Graham with a clear view of my chest. He didn't disappoint. His gaze delved down my blouse, his pupils dilating. He licked his lips before refocusing his attention on his chopsticks.

The man was great for my ego. I knew men liked to look at me. I'd made a living off of it, in fact. Something about Graham's attention felt different. He was discreet about it, as if he refused to admit he liked what he saw. Perhaps it felt like a challenge to me. I *wanted* him to want me. Maybe because I respected him so much. If a man that I admired was attracted to me, did that make me a better person?

Did it make me as respectable as I considered him to be?

But I already knew the answer to that. Only if he liked the inside of me as much as the outside.

As he practiced his technique with the chopsticks, he smiled at me, a beautiful smile framed by his close-cropped beard.

"What?" I asked, smiling as well from being put on the spot. Nervous anticipation always caused me to giggle or grin, even when the situation didn't call for it.

"I have so many questions for you, but I don't want to sound like a nosy ass."

"You can ask me anything. I'm an open book."

He laid the chopsticks down on his napkin and wrapped his fingers around his water glass, turning it back-and-forth. "I haven't noticed any friends or family step forward to offer their support or check on you. Do you not have any family?"

I lowered my head, picking at my nail polish. "Everyone has a family. We all came from somewhere. But not everyone is as close as the Carricks."

His tone was gentle and sincere. "It's really none of my business. I'm just concerned for you. It's important that you have a support system when you're facing something like this."

I pasted a false, bright smile on my face and met his gaze. "Like I said, I'm an open book," I repeated, shrugging carelessly. "I'm an only child. My parents' rainbow baby. I think that's what they call it," I said, waving my hand. "They didn't expect to be able to get pregnant, and I came along as a happy surprise, late in their lives. Both of my parents are professors. They are steeped in the academia culture and come from another era. So when their rainbow baby turned out to actually be a *rainbow baby*, they were less than understanding." I tapped my nails on the table and grinned. "I'm just too fabulous for them."

Graham frowned, stroking his beard. He nodded his head in silent understanding.

"Did you have more questions?"

He grinned sheepishly. "I didn't mean for this to sound like an inquisition. I'm just so curious about you. I find you absolutely intriguing."

"Intriguing?" I asked, my face mirroring delight.

"I've never met anyone like you before. I think you might be the most interesting person I know." He winked, looking so devastatingly sexy that my stomach flipped. "How did you get into dancing?"

"I've been dancing since elementary school. I started out with ballet and tap, and then moved into jazz and hip-hop, or urban dance, they call it now. In high school, I studied interpretive dance. I also took gymnastics as a child. The classes were after school, which gave my parents more time at their jobs. They used my extracurricular activities as babysitting," I revealed, frowning. I had been involved in a lot of things in my childhood, but my parents were involved in nothing in my life. "In my senior year of high school, I snuck into a club with a friend of mine. They were featuring a burlesque show that night. I'd never seen anything like it or knew that kind of thing existed. But I was hooked from the first performance. I'd seen pole dancing and exotic dance, like you would see on the stage at a strip club, but burlesque was a whole different bag of tricks. It was a way for me to incorporate most of the styles of dance I'd learned, and also my gymnastics training. After that night, I began practicing immediately, and it quickly became my passion. I've never looked back," I said with a wave of my hand, shrugging my shoulders lightly.

Graham hung on my every word, watching me intently. That kind of single-minded intensity and focus directed at me ignited a spark in my belly. I was used to men looking at me with interest in their eyes, but what I saw in Graham's eyes was awe. He was impressed, not turned on, and the difference caused an entirely new reaction within me.

Our server delivered our plates, platters of rolls and sashimi and fried tempura. Graham's eyes widened as he took in the food, all of which was probably foreign to him.

"Where do I start?" he asked, his chopsticks hovering over the platter of tempura.

"Right there." I pointed to the nearest platter. "Those are vegetables dipped in a thin layer of batter and deep-fried. The sauce is a sweetened soy sauce. Pick one and give it a try," I suggested with a wink.

Graham chose a slice of fried sweet potato and dipped it in the sauce. He struggled with the chopsticks and dropped the piece of tempura in the ramekin before getting a hold of it again, and popping it into his mouth.

"Mmm," he moaned appreciatively. "That's really good." Next, he chose a fried mushroom, and dipped it successfully without dropping it. "Maybe I could be a fan of sushi after all," he mused.

"I cannot declare you a fan until you try something that isn't deep fried," I teased.

Boldly, he positioned his chopsticks around a slice of eel roll. "This is cooked, right?"

I nodded, grinning with anticipation as I watched him bring it closer to his mouth. With wide, comical eyes, he popped it between his lips. I laughed at the myriad of expressions that danced across his face as he chewed. With his nose scrunched adorably, eyes looking unsure, he swallowed, his expression going blank.

"Well?"

"I like it," he declared, reaching for another piece.

"Don't tell my boys, though. I have a reputation to maintain."

"Beer and wings?"

"Absolutely," he confirmed, grinning.

My phone rang, and I grabbed it from my purse and checked the screen. I didn't recognize the number.

"Excuse me while I answer this, it might be about my case," I explained to Graham.

He smiled and nodded as I answered the phone.

"Hello? Yes, this is Kelley Michaelson speaking... Hello, Detective. Yes, I remember meeting with you... Um, sure. Not a problem. I'll stop by as soon as I can... You, too, thanks." I hung up and shoved the phone back into my purse.

"Was that the detective handling your case?"

"It was. Detective Vallejo. She wants to examine the gifts Steven sent me. I'll need to run by my apartment and grab them and drop them off at the station."

Graham's eyes bugged out. "He sent you gifts?"

I nodded, lowering my gaze down to my half-empty plate. Looking back, it was easy to connect the dots and see how things didn't add up.

"He used to leave them at the dance studio for me while I was in my class."

"Kelley."

"I know, I know. I should have reported him long ago. I didn't see the danger."

"No, you didn't *want* to see the danger because you have a soft heart. You give people trust that they haven't earned. But it's nothing to be ashamed of. Come on, I'll drive you by your apartment, and then we'll go to the station."

"You really don't mind?"

He smiled softly and wiped his mouth on his napkin. "The only thing I mind is sitting here wasting time while that man is running around free, a threat and a menace to you and the rest of society."

I tried to protest when Graham paid the check, but he just laughed it off, insisting I could pay the next time.

He was a terrible liar.

3

GRAHAM

MY BLOOD PRESSURE rose with each block we passed. Every mile brought us closer to the worst part of town. When we pulled up in front of his building, a crumbling stucco structure painted tan with a brown roof that was missing more shingles than it still retained, I hesitated to even let him out of the truck. There was no landscaping, just red dirt, overgrown weeds, and rocks. The asphalt in the parking lot was cracked, and I had to dodge several potholes to avoid a flat tire.

Kelley looked sheepish, avoiding my eyes. "I'll be back in a jiffy. You can just wait here."

Like hell I would. There was no way he was going anywhere out of my sight. Not around this dump.

He reached for the door handle, and I laid my hand on his sleeve. "I go where you go."

I followed him out of the truck and up the stairs to the second floor. It did not escape my notice that the handrail was loose. And rusted. Kelley stopped three doors down and dug his key out of his pocket.

"Can you please just wait here? There's no need to come inside. It'll only take me a minute."

"That's not—"

Kelley's hand covered his heart, and he swallowed. "I know it's not the nicest place, but I work really hard to afford what little I have. I'm not ashamed of where I live, although I'm not exactly proud of it either. But it would put me at ease if you could just wait outside."

I almost let it go. *Almost.* My fingers closed around his thick biceps, my face pulling into an intense frown. "Hey, I didn't always live in a big, fancy house. I grew up just a few blocks from here. I struggled. Every month. I watched my mother struggle. There's nothing wrong with living modestly. Don't ever mistake me for somebody who judges." *I just want better for you.* I wisely swallowed those words.

He popped up on his tippy toes and pressed a glossy kiss to my cheek. "Thank you," he whispered in my ear.

Kelley disappeared through the door, shutting it behind him, but at the last minute, I stopped it with my foot before it could fully close. Just in case he needed me and called out and I couldn't hear. I leaned against the wall to bide my time. There was absolutely no fucking way he would ever be returning here. When the time came, I would help him find a better place to live, a safer place. It was a miracle he hadn't been raped in the laundry room already. Or had his apartment broken into. Hell, he could stay in my house and rent a room from me as long as he wanted. But returning here to this shit hole was not an option.

I poked my head through the door and the scent of

lavender assaulted my nose, and I smiled, thinking how perfectly it suited him. "Grab some clothes," I called out. Hell, grab everything. Because it would be a cold day in hell before I let him return for good.

He stepped through the door minutes later, carrying a large duffel bag over his shoulder and the handles of a large paper shopping bag in his grip.

"Did you grab clothes?" I asked, hoping he'd taken everything.

"A few things. I can always come back later. With any luck, they'll catch him soon."

"Kelley, it's not an imposition on me to bring your things into my home. I'm sure it would make you feel more comfortable there if you were surrounded by familiar things. Go back in and grab another bag of your stuff. I'll wait."

He conceded with a nod and ducked back inside, returning minutes later with another bag. I took it from his grip along with the shopping bag and carried everything to my truck.

"Promise me you will never come back here without me. I wouldn't doubt this guy knows where you live."

His beautiful blue eyes rounded, glossy pink lips parting in shock. "You really think so? It never occurred to me."

"He knows where you work, where you dance, why wouldn't he know where you live? All he would need to do is follow you home one night."

When he was seated in the car, strapped into his seatbelt, he looked back at the building one last time. Regret and apprehension reflected in his expression. I didn't blame him one bit. It may not be a palace, but it was home to him, and now he felt unsafe there. As he should. And not just because his attacker was on the loose. It unsettled a person to feel as if they had no roots, no home base, and I vowed to make my home feel like his for as long as he wanted to remain there.

THE SMELL of roasted garlic and chicken wafted through the house, and even in my bedroom, I could smell it. It made my mouth water and my stomach rumble. I unwrapped the towel from around my hips and used it to dry my dripping hair. He was at it again. In his attempt to burn off his nervous energy, he was turning himself into a maid, and it had to stop. I couldn't have him thinking he had to earn his keep in order to stay here.

Grabbing a T-shirt from my dresser, I pulled it over my head, shoved my legs into a pair of sweats, and padded barefoot down the hall.

"Kelley Michaelson! Put down the casserole dish and step away from my kitchen. That's an order," I called out.

He stomped out of the kitchen with his hands on his hips, glaring at me as I settled into the couch. "Don't you order me around, Graham Carrick! I'll cook if I want to. Since when does feeding myself exceed my guest privileges?"

Fucking-A, his blue eyes danced with fire, and that sassy hand-on-the-hip thing was making my dick hard. He looked like an avenging housewife with his apron and oven mitts over a teal and white striped and very fitted jumpsuit. Where on earth did this man shop at?

"I didn't say you were exceeding your guest privileges. Of course, you can feed yourself. What I meant was, I don't want you to feel obligated to make dinner, especially for me. You don't owe me anything for staying here. You should be taking it easy. You're under a lot of stress."

Some of the anger bled out of his expression, and his features relaxed and softened. "Oh. Well, why didn't you just say so then?" He dropped his hands from his hips and removed his mitts. "If it makes you feel better, I'll let you order takeout tomorrow night." With a wink and a sassy swish of his hips, he returned to the kitchen.

A moment later, as I was flipping through the TV channels, he reemerged, carrying a glass casserole dish in his mitted hands. "Dinner's ready," he informed me, placing the dish on a hot pad in the center of my dining room table. It was then that I noticed it was decked out with candles and proper place settings. The dining room was part of the open floor plan of my living room, but since I rarely ever used it, it had escaped my attention.

"We're eating in here?" I asked, getting up from the couch to join him.

Kelley removed his mitts and took a seat next to mine. "I know it seems like a little much for a weekday casserole dinner." He shrugged his perfectly chiseled shoulders. "You didn't see the inside of my apartment, but I'm sure you can imagine there isn't much room for a dining table. I always thought if I had a larger place, I would have a table like this." His eyes roamed the length of the black walnut table lovingly.

He reminded me of a housewife straight out of the sixties, with his jumpsuit, heels and apron. "So, eating on the couch in your studio apartment isn't fulfilling your June Cleaver fantasies?"

Kelley smiled sheepishly, touching the pearls around his neck. "Not so much," he admitted. "I know it probably feels weird for you to sit here and eat. There really isn't much reason for you to use this table when you eat alone most nights. But maybe, while I'm here, it might be nice to make use of it."

I looked at him. Really looked at him. I saw a gorgeous man with an exquisite smile, who wanted to share a delicious dinner he cooked for me while carrying on an interesting conversation. My life had definitely taken a drastic turn in a matter of days, from boring to extraordinary.

"You're right, it might be very nice," I agreed.

Kelley served the casserole, piling a heaping portion of chicken and vegetables onto my plate. It smelled amazing and looked even better. Was there anything this man couldn't do well?

"I'm performing tomorrow night at the bar. You should come and see my show."

Like I was going to let him anywhere out of my sight.

"What makes you think I haven't seen it?"

He lowered his fork, looking surprised with his wide eyes and parted lips. "You have? When?"

Smirking, I answered, "A while back, after you first

started. I came into the bar to talk to Shannon and stayed for a drink. I caught a glimpse of your routine."

I would leave out the part about how much it affected me. The fire that pooled in my gut as I watched him work the stage, wearing practically nothing, just enough to tease a man. I watched him far longer than I should have, and when I got home, his routine was burned into my mind all night long, and for several weeks afterward, I may or may not have pleasured myself to the memory several times.

"And," he prompted, "what did you think?"

I covered my smile by wiping my mouth with my napkin. "You're a professional. Very energetic. Very...flexible."

At that point, there was no hiding my smile. Not with the look he gave me, as if he doubted every word I spoke. "What?" I asked, laughing. "You know you're good. And you know what people are thinking when they watch your performance. Stop fishing for compliments."

He twisted his mouth, shaking his head. "I wasn't fishing for compliments," he mocked. "I was genuinely interested in your opinion."

I laid my fork down, studying him. "And why would that matter so much to you?"

A faint blush tinted his finely sculpted cheeks. "Because I admire and respect you."

Suddenly, the playful atmosphere had taken a decidedly intimate turn. Kelley swallowed, and I could tell he was nervous as I watched his throat bob.

"Did you want to know my opinion of your routine, or you as a person?"

"My routine," he said, evading the truth.

"Your routine is second to none. I'm sure you work very hard to be that good. But you as a man are incomparable. I've met a lot of guys, but none like you. None of them measure up to your quality." He stared at me, open-mouthed and in awe, and I covered his hand with mine. "You, Kelley Michaelson, are in a class of your own."

I removed my hand, and he brought his up to his chest to cover his heart as he swallowed. "I don't know if all of that is true, but it's the finest compliment I've ever received." His whispered "Thank you" sounded wholly sincere.

He was quiet after that, and I noticed his eyes looked a little wetter. I was positive he received bucket-loads of compliments on a daily basis, about his looks or his body, or even his dancing ability. But I wondered from his reaction just how many compliments he received about who he was on the inside. What his heart was made of. I wasn't sure many people cared to look that deep, but how could they not see it? His goodness shone like a beacon in a dark sky. It was unmistakable.

4

KELLEY

I GRIPPED the wooden barre mounted to the wall and raised my left leg high, wrapping my arm around my extended knee and pulling it in tightly to my chest as my toes pointed past my ear. My eyes found him in the mirrored wall, but he wasn't looking at my face. His gaze was focused on my groin. With my legs spread wide in a vertical split, the bubblegum pink lycra leggings clung to my bulge obscenely. I smiled to myself, feeling pleased and maybe even a little giddy.

Graham was a gorgeous man, more raw sex appeal than classically handsome. His thick dark hair was cut short with about an inch or two of length on top and peppered with silver. I thought it made him look distinguished. His scruffy close-cropped beard was mostly still dark, almost black, with lighter gray strands blended around his full peach lips. But his eyes, bright green like a meadow of clover, stood out against all that dark and brooding sexiness like a sore thumb. From what I could see of his body from the outline of the tight T-shirts he favored, he was broad-shouldered and broad-chested, and his stomach was still relatively flat. All that and a firm ass, too.

Yeah, having his eyes on me felt great. I was a natural flirt, but I didn't do it with everyone. Graham felt safe. He wasn't going to act like a skeezy perv because I winked and smiled at him. Many men assumed that because I danced on stage and wore lingerie, it meant I was down to be sexually assaulted. Rape play wasn't one of my kinks. Just because I liked wearing pretty things didn't give men a green light to let their hands and scruples roam free.

In fact, the only reason I even felt comfortable having a drink at the bar after completing my performances was because Rory had kept an eye out for me. He was another one I felt safe with. It was no surprise he was Graham's best friend. They had a lot in common.

I turned toward the barre, dropping my leg until my foot rested on top of it, and stretched my hamstring. Another glance at the mirror showed me he was still checking me out, this time my ass. I smiled as I bent at the waist, popping my backside out and rounding my cheeks for his benefit. Discreetly, he arranged his junk, and I laughed silently. The man knew how to stroke my ego without even trying. I made a mental note to purchase him a pair of compression briefs so he didn't embarrass himself in front of my class.

They began to file in just as I wrapped up my warm-up, and I waved and greeted the familiar faces. I sipped from my water bottle as they rolled out their mats and settled in, and then I was leading them through the opening meditation and stretch. For me, yoga wasn't just about treating my body good. It was about mental health. The meditation centered and calmed me, the stretching of my muscles felt like a release of stress and tension, like I was letting it all go, out of my body, out of my mind and my soul, so as not to carry it with me all week long. When I left my class, I felt lighter...freer. Happier. With the unbelievable amount of anxiety I'd been dragging behind me the last few days, I was afraid I wouldn't be able to relax and be an effective instructor today. It was only because of Graham's solid presence that made me feel safe enough to unwind and get into the right mindset to heal my soul.

I had him to thank for so many things lately.

He just kept showing up for me. Like a guardian angel.

I spied him in the mirror again, dark brows drawn down tight, mouth pulled into a thin line. He looked more like an avenging angel. He was on edge, worried my stalker would show up.

I owed Graham a huge debt of gratitude that I had no idea how to repay.

Well, I might have a few ideas, I thought, smiling to myself.

After class, we walked to the end of the block to grab smoothies from the Apple Blossom Café. Again, Graham was out of his element when it came to ordering, so I stepped in to help. He chose a table outside along the sidewalk, and I toyed with my straw, hoping to draw his attention to my mouth. Naturally, he looked, sending a warm rush of excitement through my body.

"So, you're really good at that bendy stuff. I'm impressed."

I couldn't help but laugh. "That bendy stuff is called yoga." I reached for his cup without giving him a chance to protest. "I'm dying for a taste of yours."

My fingers covered his, and he pushed the cup in my direction, without removing his hand. Leaning forward, I wrapped my glossy lips around his straw and hollowed my cheeks as I slurped. His eyes grew big and round, fixated on my mouth. When I pulled the cup away, I gave him a flirty wink and a smile, and licked my lips clean, but slowly, drawing it out as he stared.

The way he responded to me, like he was awed instead of chasing me, made my entire body flush with desire. I wanted to get on my knees for him, right here on this sidewalk, and show him the effect he had on me. Every little reaction I garnered from him felt like the sexiest foreplay.

I would let this man fuck me in a heartbeat if I wasn't convinced it would complicate things between us.

But flirting was one thing. It was practically harmless. Making moves was a whole other beast, and Graham seemed to be keeping his hands to himself. Which I respected.

"Would you like to try mine?" I held out my smoothie in offering, but he declined, shaking his head.

"I bet it tastes delicious," he lied with a twinkle in his eye, "but I don't drink anything green. It's unnatural."

"It's vegetables! It couldn't be any more natural," I said, laughing.

He shuddered dramatically. "What time do you need to be at the lounge?"

"By eight. I go on at eight-thirty."

"We have time to head home first if you want."

Home. Every time he said that word, so casually and inclusive, my chest warmed. I never referred to my studio as home. It was just... My studio, my apartment. Temporary shelter.

I felt so comfortable there, and it surprised me how quickly his home had become familiar to me. Maybe because it felt so incredibly safe. But it wasn't because of his fancy security system. It was Graham. His strength and his fierce protective instincts. I had shown up there with a cart full of baggage and a stalker to boot, but he never made me feel unwanted. Not once had I felt like I was walking on eggshells, infringing upon his privacy. Graham went out of his way to make me feel at home there, and I truly did.

THE SIZE of the crowd gathered to see my performance grew every week. With my stalker still at large, it made Graham extremely nervous. He barely even glanced at the front end of the bar. His attention was focused solely on the lounge. He stood with his arms crossed over his considerable chest, wearing the darkest scowl that only meant business, daring someone to approach him—or me.

I'd changed into a black ensemble tonight to match

my choice of music. The long satin gloves covered my arms to my elbows. I wore a bustier that stopped just below my nipples, which were covered in glittery star-shaped pasties, and a matching G-string. My long legs were sheathed in thigh-high fishnet stockings, and a top hat sat on my head. I felt sophisticated and sexy as I danced to a classic George Michael song.

It was almost disappointing that Graham hadn't turned around to watch as I completed an impressive backflip and landed in a split.

Try doing that in stiletto heels and see how you fare.

I'd worked up quite a sweat, and by the time I finished my fourth song, my skin was flushed and dewy, and my heartbeat raced deliciously. I loved the feeling of getting worked up on stage, muscles stretched and burning as I pushed myself to the limits of my endurance. All while smiling like it was effortless and flirting with the crowd.

Dancing was a challenge, and to me, it was an addiction I never wanted to recover from. For my last song, I slowed things down a bit, slithering sensuously across the stage to '*I Want To Sex You Up*' by Color Me Badd. Although tense and on alert, Graham seemed pulled by a magnetic force to turn and watch, his eyes raking down my body as I slinked closer to him. The attraction between us, like an invisible thread pulled taut, felt so potent that he seemed hypnotized, unable to look away or catch his breath.

I only had eyes for him, as if we were the only two people in the room, and I was performing solely for his pleasure. Someone in the crowd whistled, breaking the connection, and I finished my performance by sliding off my glove and tossing it to Graham. He caught it in one hand and brought it close to his face. I imagined he was smelling it, checking the satin for traces of my scent, but I had a ridiculous imagination.

Graham tucked it into his back pocket and headed for the side stage, ducking behind the curtain to join me in the back hallway.

"Great job! You were incredible."

I pulled a towel out of my duffel bag and patted my chest dry, calling attention to my sparkly nipples, drawing his gaze. I removed the pasties and dried them slowly, although it was unnecessary, and watched his face as he eyed my body. His gaze dropped as I lowered the towel, and I knew he was looking at the shiny bulge my dick made tucked behind the thin black satin panties. I had to wear the tightest fitting pair I could find in order to minimize flopping on stage, and a wardrobe malfunction. But if he kept staring at it much longer, a wardrobe malfunction was going to be unavoidable.

Graham coughed and shook his head, stroking his beard to divert his attention, and I bit back my satisfied smile. He was absolutely adorable.

All too soon, I gave up the pretense with the towel and slipped a pair of black joggers over my fishnets. A cropped gray sweatshirt covered my bustier, and I traded the heels for a pair of black running shoes.

"Can I get you something to drink?"

"How about an ice-cold Arnold Palmer?"

I just wasn't in the mood for alcohol tonight. But a frosty lemonade and iced tea combo would do the trick. I warmed a seat at the bar for another hour while Graham kept an eye on the crowd until they began to thin out. There were only a handful of customers left when he decided to call it a night.

The humid air enveloped me in a warm hug when I stepped outside. With his hand pressed to the small of my back, Graham escorted me to his truck. He was parked in the back of the lot, and as we crossed the rows of empty spots, a car pulled out of a space and headed toward us, its bright headlights blinding me.

I panicked and froze, my fingernails digging into the palm of my hand. As the car came closer without slowing down, I cried out, terrified, and closed my eyes, positive it was going to slam into us. But at the last second, Graham yanked me aside, just as the car screeched to a loud halt.

"Jesus Christ, Kelley."

He pulled me tight against his chest, wrapping his arms around my back. The driver cursed at us as he drove past, slamming on the gas and burning rubber out of the lot.

"You're okay." His voice was soft, but urgent in my ear. I shook off the panic as my senses returned.

"I thought he was going to hit me."

"It wasn't him." He squeezed me tighter, his fingers trailing down my spine, past the hem of the sweatshirt, over my bare skin. "Probably just a customer who had too much to drink tonight."

His breath tickled my ear, and I leaned into him. "Thank you for looking after me." I pushed my face into his chest, inhaling his leather and honeysuckle scent.

That was one hell of a combination for a cologne. It made me want to lick him.

"Always," he rasped, and I wondered if he meant it, or if he was just placating me.

"I feel foolish now, thinking every car is going to run me down." I shook my head as I reluctantly pulled away from his embrace, still feeling a bit shaken.

Graham took my chin in his grasp and looked into my eyes. "Don't you dare feel foolish. You have every right to your feelings. It makes perfect sense that the headlights would have triggered you. That man had no business driving that car just now."

"I'm just glad you were here. To keep me safe."

"So am I. Don't you worry, I've got my eye on you."

His eyes continued to burn into me, his mouth just an inch from mine. I could feel his warm breath on my lips. My heart beat painfully hard and a jittery feeling swirled in my gut. Adrenaline and lust. I was high on it as I closed my eyes, waiting to taste his kiss.

But it never came.

Exhaling on a harsh sigh, he backed away, took my arm, and led me to the truck, where he opened the passenger door for me and buckled me into my seatbelt. It was the first time anyone had done that for me. Probably because I always came across as being so independent. But now that I considered it, it felt...nice. I wouldn't mind a bit of coddling now and then.

Especially from Graham.

I contemplated the heated moment we shared the entire ride home. Graham was content to remain silent, probably lost in his own thoughts. And when we walked into the house, I was disappointed that he went straight to his room, closing the door behind him.

I felt like he was shutting me out. But that was ridiculous. I was making more of the situation than was necessary. He was probably just showering.

Except, he never came back out.

5

GRAHAM

MY DICK HAD REMAINED HALF hard since the incident by the truck.

The incident? Who was I kidding? I'd almost kissed him!

His red-stained lips had been less than an inch from mine. And when he closed his eyes, I knew...he wanted it. Was waiting for it.

And I panicked.

Buried under the weight of self doubt and good judgment.

What the fuck was I thinking? What a fucking mess. As soon as we arrived home, I went straight for my room to grab a shower, hoping to relieve the tension in my groin. But as I stood there, stroking my dick with a soapy hand, my mind kept wandering back to *the incident*. Back to ruby lips and long fluttering blond lashes. The weight of him in my arms, solid and warm. His sweet perfume—he smelled like a damn tropical vacation—like paradise.

Those lacquered blood-red nails digging into my forearm, gripping me, drawing me in closer to his mouth.

Fuck! I shot ropes of thick white cum across the tiled wall of my shower. I didn't want to indulge my fantasies of him. He didn't deserve to be mentally ogled just because he was a beautiful man.

A sexy man. Sinfully sexy.

Jesus Christ, Graham.

I scrubbed my face under the hot spray, hoping to cleanse my mind, but every time I closed my eyes, all I saw was him. I could still smell him. Good God, I was a sick fuck.

I climbed out of the shower, toweled off, and strode into my room naked, grabbing a pair of briefs from my dresser drawer. As I slipped into them, I glimpsed the patio light come on through my bedroom window, and tiptoed through the darkness to peer out, knowing he couldn't see me shrouded in the shadows. Kelley was soaking in the hot tub, buried up to his chin in bubbles. The steam wafted over his face, making his cheeks flush pink. I couldn't help but wonder what he wore beneath the surface of the water.

For the last week, he had made a habit of soaking almost daily to alleviate soreness in his muscles after his performance or a workout. Sometimes, I joined him. Tonight, it was a risk I couldn't afford to take.

Stepping away from the window, I drew the curtain closed to give him privacy. The last thing I needed was to sit here and creep on him while he tried to relax. I climbed into bed and grabbed my tablet, but I quickly lost interest in scrolling social media. I checked out the specs for the new Roadster that Harley Davidson was about to unveil but wasn't impressed.

Fuck, my dick was still half-hard, probably because Kelley was still half on my mind. I switched to a porn site and pulled up a video of one of my favorite models. In one hand, I held the tablet, and in the other, I held my dick, stroking slowly as I waited for the movie to warm me up.

It didn't, though.

I slammed the tablet down on the mattress and glared at the ceiling, pissed off at myself and the porn star. This wasn't working. I took a couple of slow deep breaths and changed tactics, going back to social media again. Since I'd followed Kelley on YouTube last week, his backlist of videos kept showing up in my feed. I clicked on one I hadn't seen yet and was pleasantly surprised to see it was one of his workout videos.

God, he looked incredibly hot. Kelley wore a black, cropped compression top and a pair of black running shorts that barely covered the top of his thighs. They were short and loose. Even in athletic clothes, he had a full face of makeup on. The contrast between muscled bodybuilder and femme fatale had my dick all the way hard again. I tugged my briefs down under my balls and freed my cock, stroking lightly as I watched him straddle a padded bench and load weights onto a metal bar. When he bent forward slightly, the tiny shorts rode up his ass, pulling taut between his generous cheeks.

Christ. I couldn't stop myself from wishing I was his spotter. He began to curl free weights, warming up his sculpted biceps, and my mouth watered as he flexed, the muscles swelling with each repetition.

There was no excuse for what I was about to do. Nothing I could say to justify myself morally. Reaching over the side of the bed for my discarded jeans, I grabbed his black satin glove from the back pocket and brought it to my nose, inhaling traces of his sweet perfume. Thank God, he hadn't asked for it back. I slid my hand inside the satin and wrapped my gloved fingers around my cock, squeezing a little harder than I had before. I tightened my grip over the swollen head, drawing out a drop or two of precum, and spread it over the tip of my dick to ease the glide of my hand.

In the video, Kelley laid down flat on the bench and spread his thighs wide, bracing his feet on the floor. There wasn't much I couldn't see between his legs. Pale blond peach fuzz, a glimpse of hot pink underwear. He panted harshly as he pumped the bar, lifting it up over his chest again and again. My stomach warmed, and I felt the heat spread lower. Tension was building slowly in my balls, and it felt so damn good drawing it out as I listened to him countdown from fifteen.

Ten... nine...

I stroked faster, flicking my hand over the tip. The texture of the wet satin felt incredible gliding over my sensitive skin.

Eight... seven...

My balls tingled as they drew up tight to my body.

Six... five...

I closed my eyes, focusing on the buildup, the pleasure and the heat that was cresting, making my stomach spasm.

Four... three...

The ringtone on my phone echoed like a gunshot through the silence, and I jumped, fumbling the tablet and dropping it. I accidentally touched the screen and inadvertently clicked something, losing his video all together.

Fuck! I reached for the phone with my non-gloved hand before it could ring again.

"What?" I growled in frustration.

"Jeez, Pops. Someone is feeling grumpy and scowly."

There was a damn good reason I was scowly. I'd been in a constant state of arousal for a week straight and the only way to get any relief made me feel ashamed of myself.

"Did you call for a reason, Shannon? Or just to bust my chops?"

"I called to tell you that your shipment of paper products for the Bar and Grille is going to be delayed by two days. I informed your manager on duty. He said he should have enough to make it until then. Is everything all right? Am I interrupting something?"

You sure as fuck are.

"No. Just a long night. Was there something else you wanted before I go?"

Shannon's easy chuckle sounded like he was in no hurry to get off the phone. He knew he was interrupting something and aimed to drag it out as long as he could to annoy me.

"You got company, Pops?"

"You know I don't, smartass. Are you finished?"

"Sure thing. I'll let you get back to whatever it is you were doing before I called."

I had a feeling he knew exactly what I was doing. How was it possible that at fifty-three years old, my son could still embarrass me?

"Great. Maybe next time, send a text instead of calling. Bye."

I hung up without waiting for his reply and picked up my tablet, but I was no longer in the mood to hunt down his video and resume where I left off. I got up and walked over to the window to peer out the curtain. The hot tub was empty, and the lights were shut off. Kelley had gone to bed.

Disappointment streaked through me, chased by a shot of loneliness. As much as I enjoyed his company, I should never have invited him to stay here. His safety was paramount, but now I was the one in jeopardy. At risk of making a fool of myself over a much, much younger man. A man who was so far out of my league, we were playing different sports altogether. I needed to get a grip on myself and straighten out my priorities. And right now, my priority was Kelley's safety, not finding out if the lipgloss he wore tasted like strawberries.

GODDAMN, there was no reprieve from him. Nowhere I could escape to within my own house, where I could forget for five minutes how extraordinarily attractive and ridiculously sexy the man was. I went in search of coffee, only to find a plate filled with fresh cut fruit and a breakfast burrito that I assumed included some sort of kale or something healthy along with my eggs.

He was at it again, dressed in one of his skimpy lycra leotards, bent over his yoga mat in a position that was guaranteed to make my morning wood last all day.

Today, he added rainbow leg warmers to his outfit and a terry cloth headband and matching wristbands. He reminded me of Jane Fonda, or Suzanne Somers, back when they did Jazzercise videos in the 1980s.

No matter what Kelley did, he dressed for the occasion. To the nines. Everything he did, he did with his whole heart. Every day was an adventure in fashion, and I couldn't wait to guess what he had planned for the day according to the clothes he had chosen with care.

If he was making dinner, he wore a strand of pearls around his neck, and an apron tied around his waist. He seemed to favor the fancy oven mitts instead of just grabbing a kitchen towel to remove hot things from the oven like I did. And he was a master at mixing seasonings to make the food taste better than anything I'd ever created in that kitchen.

When Kelley cleaned the house, he pushed his hair back from his face with a soft cotton headband and donned baggy overalls with a fitted crop top beneath. Somewhere in my closet he had unearthed a pair of pink rubber gloves that covered his arms up to the elbows.

But my favorite by far was when he dressed for the pool. If he were exercising and swimming laps, he wore a tiny, hot pink speedo with white polka dots. I'd never seen anything like it. Especially not when he added a matching swim, cap and goggles. If he was relaxing in a lounge chair in the shade, playing on his tablet, he wore a bikini. An honest to God women's bikini. With little triangles over his nipples, and bowties across his hips. He topped off the ensemble with a wide-brimmed straw hat and oversized sunglasses, and a sheer robe that covered nothing.

The sight of Kelley in a bikini made the girls on the covers of the Sports Illustrated swimsuit magazine look like frumpy cows.

It boggled my mind to think how he fit all of that in an oversized duffel bag. It must've been the equivalent of the clown car, where the space inside was endless. His creative ensembles checked every one of my fantasy boxes, most I wasn't even aware I had.

Never in a million years would I have guessed anybody would look sexy in baggy overalls. My balls were turning blue from walking around in a constant state of arousal, and I felt ashamed of myself for panting after a man who was twenty-eight years younger than me. Christ, he was younger than my son and all my nephews.

Besides the fact that I knew nothing about relationships, I refused to make a fool of myself by letting him know I was interested or attracted to him. I felt like a perverted old letch, drooling over this perfect and pretty specimen of a man. I was nothing better than a step above a grease monkey but in a cleaner pair of jeans.

Kelley, he was...exquisite.

Yeah, I had put him up on a pedestal. Like ten miles high, where no other man could touch him. Kelley Michaelson was in a class of his own, and men like me were only good for one thing in his world, compliments and tips.

Indeed, I was a hypocrite. I was guilty of the same offense as Rory was. But worse. Because my crush on my houseguest had eleven years on his relationship with my nephew. Like I was going to let that bastard ever beat me at anything. Ha!

I carried my plate and my coffee to the couch and hid my face and wandering eyes behind my newspaper, pretending to read the headlines like I did every morning, as I listened to him pant and stretch.

"I'm going to visit Rory today. Check up on him and see how he's doing. I'd like for you to come with me. I don't like leaving you here alone."

He flopped to his mat in a graceful heap. "Are you sure? I feel so responsible for his injury. It's hard for me to face him, especially while he's still in so much pain."

I laid my paper down and looked at him. "Kelley, I've told you over and over, you have nothing to feel guilty for. Rory would love to see you and know that you're doing well. Plus, you can distract him while I check up on my nephew."

Kelley smiled and reached for a towel to pat his damp skin dry. "Let me just hop in the shower real quick and I'll be ready to go."

6

KELLEY

RORY'S HOME WAS BEAUTIFUL, like Graham's. Again, I was reminded of all they had accomplished in the two decades they had on me that I had yet to achieve. Rory settled on the sofa with his legs propped up on his coffee table. The white bandage that covered his stab wound glared at me, making me feel self-conscious for the part I played in having caused his injury. But he was so warm and welcoming, and Carlisle offered me a glass of iced sweet tea, and little by little, I began to relax.

Graham and Rory fell easily into a conversation I couldn't follow about motorcycles and the running of the bars, which left Carlisle and I to talk amongst ourselves. He was a kind soul, always asking after my well-being, offering me a complimentary drink on the house after each performance. I knew he was a fan, after all, he was the one who had hired me to dance at the lounge.

"Is he really doing well, or just faking for my benefit?"

Carlisle laughed, waving me off. "Rory? Faking it?

Never. He's healing remarkably well. He's a fighter, and he does wear a brave face, but also, he's tough as nails. Don't you worry about him."

"Because that's *your* job?" I teased with a coy smile.

His cheeks actually pinked. Adorable. "I'm doing my best."

"It must be more than enough because you both look happy. He keeps looking over here, by the way, at you."

His blush turned into a full-fledged smile. "Is he? You know, I never saw myself with a man. Especially not one so completely opposite of me. But I highly recommend it. And my uncle is so much like him it's scary. I guess that's why they're friends."

He stared expectantly at me, waiting with a pregnant pause for my reaction. "Are you trying to make a subtle point?" I smiled, amused.

"Maybe not so subtle. I'm just saying, if ever you needed someone you could trust and rely on, there's no one better than my uncle. He's a good man."

"And a single man," I pointed out, following his lead.

"That, too," he winked playfully. "I'm sorry. I know you're having a terrible time right now, and I'm playing matchmaker instead of listening. I'm horrible."

I patted his knee reassuringly. "You aren't. I'm trying to compartmentalize the stress. Stick it in a room in the back of my mind and lock the door. I don't know the man who attacked me, and I'm not upset for him about whatever consequences he has to face for what he's done. That's the part that I'm most upset about. He's hurting people I care about. Making them go out of their way to keep me safe. I'm so grateful to both of them—" my eyes landed on the two men seated comfortably on the couch, deep in conversation, "—for looking after me. I wish I knew how to even the score in return for all they've done." Graham's eyes found mine, and he smiled. My heart fluttered like a moth spreading its wings, taking flight inside my chest.

Carlisle followed my gaze. "Oh, I bet I can think of something appropriate," he suggested, laughing.

"Don't get your hopes up. Graham hasn't given me any signals. At least, none that he plans to act on. He's just a big, strong, hot teddy bear that I like to think about when I shower."

Carlisle laughed loudly, drawing both men's attention to us. "We'll just see about that," he challenged.

WE WRAPPED UP OUR VISIT, and when we were settled in his truck, Graham suggested, "Why don't we stop by your apartment again so you can grab a few more of your things?"

He sounded so optimistically hopeful that I laughed. "How much stuff are you hoping I bring with me?"

"All of it," he said unabashedly.

"Seriously?" I was stunned because his expression had turned serious. He really meant it.

"Kelley, bring everything. If I'm being honest, I never want you to return there to live. It's not safe. Stay with me indefinitely, or until you find something better."

"It's not a hardship?"

"Hardship? Are you kidding me? You cook for me and clean better than I ever did. The house smells like lavender and citrus from your perfumes, and I'm inspired to inhabit more spaces in my house because you inadvertently draw me out of my cave."

"You must mean the garage," I joked.

"Exactly."

I didn't know what to say. I honestly felt choked with emotions I didn't want to identify. His generosity and concern felt like a ten-ton brick sitting on my chest, making it difficult to breathe.

"Can I think about it?"

"Of course. This isn't a fly-by-night offer. It stands indefinitely."

The open timeline made it easier to take a deep breath. It lessened some of the instant panic I felt at having to rely on someone's kindness in order to take care of myself properly. I hated feeling beholden to anyone for any reason. It truly wasn't Graham's intention, I believed that fully, but nevertheless, it was an old familiar soundtrack that played in my head. And on the other hand, his offer made me feel...valued...special. He wouldn't have offered to just anyone. But he'd offered it to me. It made me think the close connection I felt with him wasn't just my imagination.

He pulled the truck to a stop in front of my building. I was hyper aware of his presence behind me. His heavy boots echoed on each concrete step of the cracked staircase as he followed me up to the second floor. As soon as I cleared the stairs, I noticed something was wrong and gasped. Fear and shock had me frozen in place, much like the headlights at the bar the other night. Graham rushed around me and ran to my door. It wasn't closed all the way, and a chunk of wood had been gouged out of the door jamb. His face hardened with anger.

"Someone broke in. Go back to the truck and call 911. Hurry."

I ran down the stairs, taking them two at a time with Graham hot on my heels, and climbed into his truck, locking my door. Graham opened the driver's side door and grabbed something from under his seat while I called the police and gave them my address.

"Wait here." He raced back upstairs.

The operator kept me on the phone while we waited for the police. I watched from the cab of his truck through the window as Graham bumped the door open with his hip and raised a gun as he ducked inside, ready to fire if threatened. I couldn't believe he had a gun! It all suddenly felt so real, so precarious and dangerous. I feared for his safety more than my own, after what had happened to Rory. The two men were making a habit of defending me, which was a terrifying but novel feeling.

With my heart in my throat, I chanted under my breath over and over, "Please be safe. Please be safe. Please be safe." The police couldn't get here fast enough. What felt like an eternity later, but was likely only minutes, Graham reappeared and waved at me to come up.

I told the operator the apartment was all clear and opted to hang up, against her advice. Hesitantly, I locked his truck behind me and climbed the stairs. I was so relieved there was no one inside, and that no one had threatened his life, that I threw my arms around his neck and hugged him. Awkwardly, he patted my back, and I became self-conscious at the sudden display of affection and pulled away.

"Tell me if anything is missing. And grab everything you can, quickly. Once the police arrive, they might possibly make you wait until they clear the scene. I just want to get you out of here as fast as possible."

I glanced around, not seeing anything out of place, and moved on to my bedroom, where I grabbed an enormous beach bag and began stuffing clothes into it without stopping to coordinate my outfits. Now was not the time to worry about matching color palettes.

I felt skeeved out thinking of how that man had possibly, and quite probably, touched my clothes and intimate items. He had invaded my privacy. Tainted my home. My peace of mind was now infected with fear. I hated having to take these things with me and bring them into Graham's home. It felt like I was bringing the filth with me, like spreading the infection.

With my bag stuffed full, I treaded over to my nightstand and checked my top drawer, almost afraid of what I'd find.

Or in this case, not find.

Yup, it was gone. He'd taken my dildo. The hot pink one that vibrated.

There were several others, but I couldn't bring myself to touch them, knowing he had. Fuck it, I'd buy new ones. It was worth the expense for the peace of mind.

Graham ducked his head in my doorway. "Almost done?"

"Yeah." I followed him out of the bedroom, and he took my bag and ran it down to his truck just as the cops pulled up. Two officers, armed and eyeing Graham as if he were the suspect, spilled out of their patrol cars. I rushed down the steps to explain before things got heated. Graham must have replaced his gun when he stowed my bag because he stepped away from the truck and raised his hands in surrender.

I addressed the officer standing closest to me. "Hi, I'm the one that called you."

"Kelley Michaelson?"

"Yes sir, that's me."

"Who is he?" The officer gestured to Graham.

"He's with me. Someone broke into my apartment."

Eyeing Graham warily, he advised, "Stay here. I'll go check it out."

The second officer stayed put. Almost as if he were babysitting us. I guessed you couldn't be too careful in this neighborhood. The investigating officer paused to examine the broken lock before entering my home. It didn't take him long to clear the scene. He joined us just as the detective handling my case, Detective Vallejo, pulled up behind the other two cars and got out, approaching our huddle.

"Mr. Michaelson, It's good to see you again."

I liked her immensely. She seemed fair, impartial, and kind. She also had incredible nails, a deep shade of plum topped with a glittery clear coat that sparkled in the sunlight.

"I wish these were better circumstances. Do you think it's the same guy?"

A grim expression crossed her pretty face. "Most likely. Was anything missing?"

My cheeks flushed crimson under the layer of carefully applied blusher. I stepped closer and whispered into her ear. "My personal items. Adult toys."

She kept a straight face, God bless her, and asked, "Was that all?"

I nodded and backed up to stand closer to Graham.

"I'll look into it. I will collect fingerprints from the lock, if I can, and your nightstand. Do you have somewhere safe to stay?"

"He's staying with me. I'll give you my information in case you need to contact Kelley and can't reach him," Graham answered, reaching into his wallet and extracting a business card, which he handed to the detective.

"Thank you, Mr.—" she read the card, "—Carrick. I had a hit this morning on Steven Masters' credit card. It was local. He's somewhere nearby. Please don't return here alone until it's safe."

Again, I nodded because words couldn't fit past the lump in my throat.

"I'll have my boys replace the lock today and secure the place until you decide what to do with it," Graham reassured me, placing his hand on my shoulder. He squeezed, and the heat from his hand eased me somewhat, but not nearly enough.

The detective and officers pulled prints, a partial they probably couldn't use, and left. We sat in his truck while waiting for Gordy and Carson to show up with a brand-new lock. Graham didn't stick around to help them out. I could tell he was anxious to get me away from there. Maybe as anxious as I was to leave it behind.

As his truck pulled out of the parking lot, a hot tear rolled down my cheek, followed by another, and then a dozen more all at once. I knew in my heart I was never going to return—not to live here—ever again.

Like any red-blooded male, my tears made Graham uncomfortable. He probably had no idea how to comfort me and it made him squirm. He grasped my hand, lacing our fingers together. It was the most familiarity he'd ever shown me. I looked at our joined hands, mine painted a fire-engine red and manicured, his bitten ragged, his cuticles caked with grease from working on his bike that morning. We were such stark opposites in every way. Yet I sometimes felt like nobody understood or appreciated me more than he did.

"We should get out of town for a bit. Go away for a few days. Clear your head so you won't be looking over your shoulder at every turn," he suggested.

"Out of town? Where would we go?"

"I have a small cabin in the mountains, about a two-hour drive from here. It's the perfect place to forget about life for a while."

I was having a hard enough time accepting his hospitality without adding a vacation to the growing list of favors he'd done for me.

"I don't know if—"

"If this is about money, don't. Don't you dare say a word." His ominous expression brooked no argument. I needed to relax. Graham didn't see it as stacking favors. He genuinely wanted to do what he thought was best for me, and it wouldn't kill me to accept an ounce of his kindness without reading too much into it.

"A vacation sounds lovely."

His bark of laughter was just what I needed to lighten the mood. "Trust me, Fancy, it's not the Ritz. It's a no-frills cabin in the middle of nowhere. Be sure to pack your bug repellant and some hiking boots."

Fancy? Was that how he saw me?

I kinda liked it. More than a little.

THERE WERE SO many spaces in Graham's lovely home that were my favorites. At the top of my list was the living room, with its vaulted ceilings and wide-open space, the floor-to-ceiling windows let in plenty of sunshine, and I could even hear the birds singing through the glass. I loved to spread my mat out on his hardwood floors and enjoy the view of the backyard as I went through my yoga routine. It was the perfect place to feel at one with the outdoors without having to endure the muggy humidity of a southern Carolina summer morning. Another favorite of mine was the patio out back. The overhang above was camouflaged beneath vines of wisteria and honeysuckle, making me feel as if I were in a Napa Valley winery. And when the sun warmed the nectar in the blossoms, the fragrance smelled incredible. Sometimes, I listened to a meditation tape, and sometimes, I just soaked up the sounds of nature, letting it balance my soul.

My tiny and cramped apartment was the last place I would ever choose to meditate or do yoga. It was nearly impossible to stretch out without banging into something.

And the atmosphere was less than Zen-like. Usually, I went to the dance studio early and incorporated my poses as part of my warm-up routine. But since living with Graham, I was able to practice every morning at home. It was the best way to start my day. Although that had less to do with the exercise and more to do with a shirtless man, staring at me from across the room as he pretended to read his newspaper.

And now, just as I had begun to settle in and feel at home here, I had to pack up and leave again. It was an illogical thought. I would be returning soon enough. The constant upheaval and change was beginning to weigh heavily on me.

"You ready?"

"Yeah. I think I have everything," I said as I hefted two duffel bags over my shoulder while balancing two more in my hands.

Graham eyed my haul and laughed to himself. His lopsided smirk was sexy as hell and made me feel a bit silly. I had overpacked way too much for a quick mountain getaway.

"Come on, Fancy. Let's hit the road."

7

GRAHAM

WE PASSED endless miles of beautiful scenery—emerald green pine trees, rolling foothills and sweeping mountains—before I pulled the truck off the rural highway and onto a dirt road that wound up the base of the mountain. The cabin was about halfway up, and there were only two ways to get to it: a big truck with four-wheel-drive, or a pack mule.

The truck bounced and jostled over the pitted road, and Kelley had a death grip on the safety handle mounted above the window, his eyes big and round with trepidation.

"Hang on, Fancy. We're not in Kansas anymore," I joked, quoting a line from the Wizard of Oz.

"Oh, that reminds me. Have I told you about the time I dressed as Dorothy for Halloween? I'll have to dig up the pictures from somewhere."

I would love to see those. I laughed to myself. He was too easy to distract. Just the idea of dressing up got him excited.

I rolled down the windows so I could breathe in the fresh pine-scented air. The cabin, and the mountain it sat on, were wild and wonderful, and I loved everything about being up here. The bewildered look on Kelley's face as he took it all in made me think that through his eyes, he saw it as more wild and a lot less wonderful than I did.

He was fucking precious.

His idea of dressing for the mountains was a black and red checkered flannel shirt, tied in a knot above his belly button, with black skinny jeans tucked into black hiking boots that looked way too designer posh to actually aid him in hiking. The real kicker was the ruby belly button piercing that flashed every time he twisted his torso. Back on the highway, I'd almost missed my exit twice because my eyes kept straying to his stomach. It was like a flashing neon sign that said, 'Check out my abs'!

I'd need to keep a close eye on him this week so he didn't hurt himself.

WE PULLED up to the cabin, and I parked the truck in the gravel drive. As I grabbed the bags from the back, I kept an eye on Kelley's face, waiting for his expressions to reveal what he thought of the place. He was horrible at schooling his features. His wide-eyed wonder made me think he wasn't necessarily looking down on it for all that it lacked, but instead, he found the whole setting completely foreign.

Wait 'till he gets a load of the inside, I thought with a snicker.

I carried all four of his bags, along with my single duffel, into the cabin, and dumped them in the only bedroom in the back. He appeared over my shoulder, peering into the room. The antique wooden bed frame was queen-sized and hand carved. I picked it up at an antique shop in the nearest town years ago when I bought the cabin. The quilt, as with all the quilts in this cabin, was handmade by my mother and worn by love and time.

A dresser and nightstand were the only other furnishings in the room. "Is this your bedroom or the guest room?"

I smiled slyly as I answered, "One and the same, Fancy."

"What does that mean?"

"It means there's only one room in this cabin. You get the bedroom, and I get the couch."

He followed me back out to the living room, which was really one big great room, although not that big, as the kitchen and dining nook were attached. All the furniture was secondhand and mismatched, but everything was made of solid wood and built sturdy to last. It wasn't magazine quality, but I thought it looked homey and comfortable.

Kelley wandered into the kitchen, and his expression faltered.

"It's not much to look at, just the basics. Not a lot of square footage to clean or fancy appliances and equipment to maintain. Just a bed, a couch, barely a kitchen, and a stream that runs behind the house full of trout. I come here to get away and relax, clear my head."

He rallied with his bright smile. "So this is your form of meditation or yoga."

"Fishing. Fishing is my yoga."

"Fishing?" His hand fluttered to his throat, and if he'd worn his pearls today, he'd be clutching them. I guessed it didn't match with his flannel lumberjack look.

"Don't tell me you've never tried it."

"Nope, never."

I closed a few inches of distance between us and stared at his mouth as his lips parted. "I guess I'll have to teach you how to hold a pole the right way," I teased.

"Like I've never heard that joke before," he said, laughing. His laughter reminded me of church bells, smooth and melodic. "As a dancer, who sometimes incorporates a pole into his routine, trust me, I've heard every pole joke ever invented."

"That sounds like a challenge. I'll have to think of something creative." I stepped around him and reached for the cupboards, opening each one and taking stock of the contents. "Will you be okay here unpacking while I run to the store? It's only a few miles from the base of the mountain. It shouldn't take me more than an hour."

"Are you sure I'm safe here?"

"Kelley, I wouldn't dare leave you alone if I didn't think you'd be safe. There's not another soul for miles around. The next closest house is at the top of the mountain, several miles up."

"I wasn't talking about safety from my attacker or

people. I was thinking more like bears and mountain lions."

I laughed loudly, the muscles in my stomach clenching as I bowed over. "You should be fine, Fancy. No mountain lions and bears. But if one comes through the door, just spray it with your perfume."

He glared, not finding the humor in my joke, which made me laugh even louder.

IT DIDN'T TAKE LONG to make my way through the little general store, the only one in town. If you could call it a town. Rook Mountain had a population of 137 people, most of them seasonal like me. Everything you needed could be found in the little mom and pop store off the side of the highway. Food, drinks and ice, gas, and basic household supplies were all sold here.

I grabbed some snacks and drinks, a bag of ice, and anything that looked healthy enough for Kelley to enjoy, and made my way back to the cabin before he became anxious about the local wildlife.

When I returned, I found Kelley in the kitchen, washing mushrooms in a metal strainer. "Where'd you get those?" I asked, hefting the bags onto the counter.

"They were growing outside around the perimeter of the cabin. And thank God for small favors, you have Internet here."

I chuckled. "I'm not a total heathen."

"Uh huh, I think it has less to do with staying connected and more to do with your need for porn."

"What makes you think I need to get it off the Internet? They sell DVDs, you know."

"Don't lie," he accused, narrowing his eyes. "I investigated and found your VHS player. And your entire VHS collection of movies. Lots of Kevin Costner and Steven Seagal, but no vintage porn. Which leads me to believe that you pay for Internet here only so you can have access to your favorite sites. I, on the other hand, used it for much more wholesome purposes. Like googling these mushrooms to see if they're edible."

"They are. Chanterelles. They're delicious. There's also a bunch of wild berries out there. The blueberries are great for snacking, but the strawberries and blackberries are too tiny. No juice, and very tart. Carlisle loves to freeze them and float them in his lemonade and iced tea."

"Do the boys come here often?"

"Often enough. My sisters use it, too."

"It's a shame it's not large enough for all of you to stay at once."

I chuffed sarcastically. "Is it? Have you ever seen us all together? It's likely the cabin wouldn't even be standing after that reunion."

We danced around each other in the tiny kitchen as we prepared dinner, constantly bumping into one another. The linguini with lemon, butter and garlic sauce was quick and simple, and made the tiny cabin smell delicious.

"Do you have an apron I can use?"

"No apron, just a dish rag."

Kelley shrugged, ever optimistic and resourceful. "No problem. I'll just take my shirt off."

Fuck, it was hot in here, and not because the kitchen was small. Kelley didn't seem to notice my eyes on him as he stirred the sauce. His broad shoulders and rippled back made my fingers itch to knead them. His thick corded biceps flexed as he stirred, but it was his chest and stomach that made breathing difficult. He was perfectly sculpted; the body of a God, and the face of an angel. If ever there was a man to tempt me from such a long, cold, dry spell, it was surely Kelley Michaelson.

After dinner, we settled on the couch to watch a movie. Where and when had he gotten the matching pajama set with pine trees and bears on them? I laughed to myself, thinking he wouldn't be caught dead not dressed appropriately for any occasion. Eventually, Kelley leaned his head back on the couch and fell asleep. I waited until the movie ended before trying to rouse him, but he refused to budge. I covered him in an old wedding ring quilt my mother made decades ago and spent the night in the bedroom.

I would be lying if I said I'd made use of the internet. Images of Kelley cooking shirtless were enough to light my fire. His smooth tanned skin and small pink nipples, the tight stomach and ruby stud in his belly button... yeah, it did the job just fine.

KELLEY SEEMED WITHDRAWN. He sat huddled on the porch swing wrapped in a quilt. Perhaps he was spending too much time in his head. There were so many changes in his life, all occurring at once, and it was no surprise that he was lost in thought. It must be weighing heavily on him. He needed a distraction. I grabbed the fishing poles and tackle box and stepped out onto the porch.

"You ready?"

He raised his head, looking confused. "Ready? For what?"

"Fishing. You promised to let me show you how to properly handle my pole."

He finally cracked a smile. "You should come with a warning label," he teased, shaking his head.

So should you, I thought. *Warning: likely to induce heart failure.*

"Hang on, I need to go change."

"What's wrong with what you're wearing?" I thought he looked fine in his rolled and cuffed boyfriend jeans and purple tank top.

Kelley tilted his head, giving me a look that said, "Really?"

"I can't wear this to go fishing. Get real." He dashed by me, leaving me standing there, confused as shit, holding the poles as I waited on him to get pretty for the fish.

I INDULGED in a selfish moment of weakness as I caged him in my arms, his back flush against my chest, showing him how to hold the fishing pole and how to cast the reel. He wore a soft pink Henley, tied in a knot above his hip to show off his belly button and the V-cut of his abs. His piercing today was a gold hoop with a tiny gold heart that dangled with each swish of his tight hips. Khaki capri chinos were rolled up over his calf to showcase gray rubber boots with pink hearts.

Where does this guy shop at?

He had the boy-next-door good looks, the body of a man who spent hours in the gym, which he did, and yet his clothes were ultra feminine. But somehow, the whole thing just worked for him. Compared to my stained jeans and Limericks Bar T-shirt, he was way overdressed, but damn if I didn't appreciate his effort.

"I think I have the hang of it. Stand back in case I snag you when I cast off."

"Cast, but not cast off. That's boating lingo." I was more worried about him snagging himself than me.

"You ever swim in this creek?"

"Nah. Too shallow, and the current is too strong."

"It's beautiful here. Very peaceful. I can see why you love it."

I stared as he reeled his line in. He was—*fuck*—he was... He made looking away difficult.

"What?" he asked shyly, aware that I was staring. "Do I have mud on my cheek or something?" He swiped his cheek, depositing a streak of mud on his otherwise clean face. I smiled. Hell, it felt like all I did lately was laugh and smile.

"Hurry up and catch me a damn fish or we're going to starve for dinner," I teased playfully.

"Oh, we're actually eating these?" He looked at the stream with revulsion, his nose adorably scrunched. "I eat fish, but I don't clean and scale them."

No shit. "Descale, you mean. Don't worry, Fancy, I'll

take care of it. I don't want you to chip your pretty manicure."

He narrowed his blue eyes but smiled, knowing I was kidding.

UNSURPRISINGLY, he didn't catch any fish. I started a fire in the pit out back and skewered a plant-based hot dog on a stick for Kelley to roast. He'd gone quiet again, lost in thought. He wasn't the only one with something on his mind, though.

"What did he take from you?" I asked, breaking the silence of the quiet night.

"Who?"

"Don't pretend like you don't know what I'm talking about. Steven Masters. What did he take from the apartment?"

"I don't know what you're talking about. Everything looked untouched."

"That's bullshit. Detective Vallejo asked you if anything was missing, and instead of saying no out loud, you tiptoed over and whispered in her ear."

"I don't tiptoe," he said haughtily.

"Yes, you do," I countered, laughing. "You tiptoe all over a stage every Friday night, and you look damn sexy doing it, too. I'll ask you again, and for the last time, what did he take from you?"

"Something personal. Not that it's any of your business."

"Oh no? You don't think so? I'm just trying to keep you safe."

"I know that, and I appreciate that more than I can explain to you."

"The only thing I want you to explain to me is what he took from you."

His cheeks heated to a rosy blush. "A toy from my nightstand."

"A toy? You mean a—"

"Yes! That's exactly what I mean."

No wonder he was reluctant to share. "What else?"

"Honestly, I don't know. Probably some panties or something. I have so many I can't keep count. And I haven't taken the time to examine my collection closely enough to discern what is missing. But I wouldn't doubt something has been taken."

I swallowed, feeling my blood pressure rise. "Great, so now he has your DNA. Lord knows what he could do with that if he has access to a lab."

Kelley blanched. "I didn't think about that. Thanks for the peace of mind."

I felt like an ass. "I'm sorry. I'm about to explode, and I'm trying to keep a tight leash on my anger."

"I can see that."

I planted my hands on my thighs and pushed to my feet. "He had no right to touch your things! No right to invade your home and your life. But of all the things he could have stolen from you, I think that pisses me off the most. What a sick fuck." I needed to calm down so as not to further upset him. "Don't worry. They're going to catch him soon. In the meantime, you're safe. We'll replace everything he touched."

"We?" He smirked, his perfectly plucked blond eyebrow arching wryly.

"You. I'll help. Financially. Or...whatever you need... from me." Jesus Christ. Every time he got me flustered, I said the stupidest shit! "I just want you to know you can count on me for anything. I'm totally invested, and I'm here for you, right by your side. You aren't alone, Kelley. Besides me, you have Rory and the boys. We all want to help. You're family now."

He swallowed hard, his throat bobbing in the warm glow of the fire, and when I saw his sapphire eyes mist, I let it drop.

8

KELLEY

THE SUN HAD SET, leaving us in darkness, illuminated by the soft glow of the fire. The light played off the silver strands in Graham's beard, making them sparkle like tinsel on a Christmas tree. Ugh! What was it about older men that drove me nuts? Something about all that maturity was so damn sexy. Especially on a guy like Graham, who didn't even know how hot he was. He was oblivious to his Daddy appeal, not that I was looking for a Daddy. But a guy could certainly pretend in the bedroom, couldn't he?

Reluctantly, I left him to put the fire out by himself while I went and showered off the smoky smell that clung to my clothes and skin. I changed into ruby-red satin sleep pants and a matching lacy camisole that showed off my nipples. Not because I was trying to look sexy for him, although it was a side effect that didn't hurt, but I just loved the way the lace rubbed against my nipples when I moved. It made me feel sensual and pretty.

I wondered how it would make Graham feel.

I joined him in the living room. He was in the process of spreading out a sheet over the couch for his bed. When he looked up, his reaction was priceless.

"Oh, come the fuck *on*," he grumbled, scrubbing his face. I guessed that summed up how he felt. I almost felt bad for him. *Almost*, I snickered to myself.

I walked over to the couch and took the pillow from him, squeezing it to my chest. "I don't want you to sleep on the couch. It sags in the middle, and it's bad for your back."

"I have an air mattress in the closet. If it gets bad, I'll blow it up."

Thinking of him blowing anything made me squirm. "I don't want you to sleep on the air mattress either. Not while I'll feel rotten for taking the whole bed."

"There's a motel two towns over. Would you rather I sleep there?"

"We should just share the bed."

"Not gonna happen, Fancy."

"Why not?"

"It's a bad idea. I've never shared a bed with anyone before. It's not just you," he said, eyeing my pajamas. "It's me."

Well, wasn't that interesting? I'd be his first? A surge of heat moved through me just imagining his big solid body warming mine throughout the long night.

"Just because we share a bed for a few hours doesn't mean anything. We're both adults."

He grabbed the pillow from me and tossed it onto the couch, moving into my space. "Is that right?"

"Uh, yes. Definitely."

Graham scoffed. "Look at you, Fancy. A man like me doesn't need that kind of..."

"That kind of what?"

"That kind of temptation."

I made the mistake of looking down at his crotch. He noticed and groaned, turning away from me. Graham sunk down into the couch, dropping his head between his hands. Well, I *went there*, and there was no backing the truck up now. Better to just roll forward, full steam ahead.

"I'm sure you've noticed that I like you. The looks that I give you, the flirting."

"You flirt with everyone," he countered, his voice muffled behind his hands.

"Okay, that's fair, but with you, it's..."

His head snapped up. "It's what?"

"I don't know, it's more. And I see the way you look at me."

His eyes rounded wide. "How do I look at you?"

"Like you want me. You do, don't you?" It was more of a statement than a question.

"It doesn't matter. You're a guest in my home."

Oh, I'd had absolutely enough of that BS. "Don't you double talk me, Graham Carrick. You tell me to make myself completely at home there, that my stay is indefinite if I want it to be, and then, when it suits your purpose, you twist it to say that I'm just a guest. Well, you can't have it both ways," I said, with my hands on my hips. I crowded his space, pointing my finger into his shoulder. "You give more mixed signals than a pitcher and his catcher." His expression changed from outraged to confused, and I amended, "Like a traffic light! Red, and then green, and then yellow. Make up your damn mind. Do you like me or not?"

He looked amused, like he wanted to laugh. I realized that I might be coming on a tad bit strong. He just got me so riled up!

"It doesn't matter. And not because you're a guest in my home."

"Of course it matters!"

"Dammit, Kelley. I've never dated a man before. Or anyone. I'm not suave or smooth like some guys. I don't do romantic gestures. I don't have a lick of game."

"What do you have, then?"

"Gray hair and a bad knee," he said, smirking.

I bent over, holding my stomach as I laughed. "You have so much more than that. Don't sell yourself short. Pickup lines and shallow compliments never worked on me, anyway."

"Oh no?"

"Don't get me wrong, I can appreciate a gorgeous man just like anyone can, but it takes more than a pretty smile and buying me a drink to land me in your bed."

He stood, meeting me at eye level. His expression no longer looked outraged or confused. He looked hungry. It was a look I was quite familiar with seeing in others. Hell, I was feeling the same way right now.

"What does it take to land a guy like you—in my bed?" His voice sounded incredibly deep and husky, making me so aware of the turn in his mood.

"Chemistry. That special spark." Graham took a step closer, his breath ghosting over my lips. "A genuine connection." I could taste the air he exhaled. Would his kiss taste as sweet?

I closed my eyes and breathed a needy sound, full of hunger and want, and brushed my lips over his. He gripped my hip, fingers digging deep into my skin. His lips were soft, and I desperately wanted him to open them so I could slip inside his mouth.

Graham pulled away from me, and when I looked into his eyes, I couldn't read him. His face was a mask of self-control.

"It's getting late," he said, making excuses for denying me. And I knew he was denying himself as well, because his fingers still had a firm grip on my hip, almost as if he wanted to pull me closer.

I didn't know what to say. My face reflected my disappointment, and I wanted to call bullshit on his excuse.

Why was he being so cowardly? What could a man as tough as him be afraid of?

I waited until he removed his hand, and then I retreated to the bedroom without a word. A thousand thoughts danced through my head as I waited for Graham to close up the house and join me. It was another hour before he slipped through the door, shutting it softly behind him. Rather than climb into the bed, he just stood there, next to the side I'd left empty for him.

"Are you planning on sleeping standing up?"

"I don't plan on sleeping at all."

I guessed I was supposed to take that as a compliment instead of an insult. "Just come on," I groused, throwing back the covers. "I don't bite."

He looked slightly disappointed. "Quit saying shit like that before I lay down next to you!"

I rolled over to face him, looking up into his eyes with a coy smile. "You aren't afraid of little old me, are you, Graham?"

He ignored my jab and slid under the covers, keeping his big body as close to the edge of the mattress as possible. I turned back over, knowing he felt too uncomfortable to lie face to face. After almost five minutes of silence, I scooted back about two inches. After another few minutes, I did it again. Graham stopped moving completely, no longer shifting to get comfortable, and I sensed he was lying on his back, holding himself rigidly still, terrified I was going to move closer. With another shuffle of my hips, I was finally close enough to feel the heat of his body. He shifted again and then flailed in a flurry of movement.

Half sitting up, I glanced over my shoulder at him. "You almost fell off the bed! Stop moving over."

"Stop scooting closer!"

With a satisfied smile on my face, I laid back down. When he stilled, I quickly closed the distance between us and reached behind me to grab his hip. "Stay. Don't you dare move."

His big rough hand covered mine. The heat of his touch traveled up my arm, making me more aware of him. If that were even possible.

Graham cleared his throat, the sound incredibly loud in the quiet room. But his voice followed in a whisper. "Kelley, what are we doing?"

"Going to sleep."

He didn't say anything more, and eventually, his hand moved to my hip. I cursed the blanket and sheet that separated his skin from mine.

"It's not you," he whispered again. "Any man would feel lucky to be me right now. I just..."

"I know. I get it." He'd hinted a few times about how many years he'd been alone, having never been in a relationship before. I was also aware how self-conscious he was about his age, compared to mine. From what I'd seen of his body, he had nothing to worry about. Only time would help him become more comfortable with me. And I wasn't going anywhere. The way I figured it, Graham was more than worth the wait.

Alone in the middle of the night, with nothing but the sound of the ticking clock on the nightstand and crickets outside the window, we were shrouded in shadows. It was the perfect setting for secrets and truths. To forge a lasting connection—a friendship—although with Graham, it would always feel like more than that.

"Who was he?" I kept my voice low, just above a whisper.

"Who?" His hand tightened on my hip.

"I don't know. You tell me."

He sighed deeply. "His name was Mike. He was a good buddy of mine for years. I had a crush."

"A crush?" I asked, slightly amused. It was hard to

picture the gruff and aloof Graham Carrick crushing on anyone.

"Something like that. I wanted him for years."

"What happened?"

"Nothing. He was straight. We rode together, he gave me a hand with looking after the boys, we hit the bars and played pool."

"And?"

"And he fell in love. With a woman. Asked me to be the best man at his wedding."

I was overcome with a sudden rush of sadness. "I'm sorry," I whispered.

"It nearly crushed me. After that, we drifted apart. He was busy with his new wife, starting a family. I just didn't want to play the game anymore."

"That's it?" That was the extent of his heart's history?

"Every now and then, I find someone to keep me company for a night or two, but then I move on. Lasting attachments aren't for me."

The sadness gathered in my throat, forming a lump. So much wasted potential to give and receive love. At least he had showered it on his boys instead of letting it wither up and die. As I lay there in the dark, replaying his words in my head, my heart expanded, and something clicked, morphing from attraction into possession. I wanted to show him what it felt like to receive the love he sought so many years ago. I wanted someone like him to claim for myself, to care for, to partner with. Just imagining having Graham by my side, not just in a crisis situation, but every day, made me feel stronger, happier. If only I could figure out how to climb his walls and slip into his heart without him realizing that was my mission.

I had spent the night with many men, always for fun, a few hours of enjoyment. But this whispered-confessions-in-the-dark thing was new for me. Never before had I shared this kind of intimacy with another man. And with each hushed word spoken, I wanted more.

9

GRAHAM

OUR CONVERSATIONS FELT QUIETER TODAY, less flirtatious, at least from Kelley. The man had the art of flirtation down to a science. Instead, our interactions felt like they carried more meaning and intention. Kelley seemed subdued, but not like before when he was weighed down with worry. Just, more introspective, maybe. I suggested we go swimming to cool off from the oppressive heat. I knew of a great spot just two miles from here, a short drive in the truck, partway down the mountain.

Compared to my baggy black swimming trunks, Kelley looked mouthwatering in a red swimsuit that I couldn't quite decide whether to label as a one piece or a bikini. The top and bottom halves were connected by strings that wound around his body and crisscrossed in a way that made me itch to trace the lines with my fingers.

I jumped in first, and he was slow to follow.

"This place is beautiful. The water is so clear." He

scanned the clearing, taking in the flowering trees and berry bushes.

"It's fed by a spring farther up the mountain."

He waded into the water, chest deep, the fabric of his swimsuit darkening to a deep blood red. His nipples hardened and poked through the material as his teeth chattered.

"I didn't realize it would be this cold considering it's so hot out."

"Usually, the spring-fed pools are chilly. The water is coming from below the ground."

He moved gracefully through the water, making me think of synchronized swimmers and aquatic dancers.

"Well, it's refreshing once you get used to it."

He dipped his head back to wet his hair, accentuating the arch of his spine, and I was grateful for the ice-cold water that helped to keep my erection at bay. I feared my shorts weren't baggy enough to disguise it.

Kelley straightened up, losing his balance as his foot slipped off a rock under the water. His arms flailed as he tried to find his footing, and I caught him in my arms.

"Mmm, much warmer now," he purred. "Thanks."

Not even the cold water could keep me from getting hard when he licked his lips and smiled like he was modeling in a toothpaste commercial. Somehow, he smelled sweet, like blooming roses, even in the water, and I found myself leaning in to catch his scent.

"Have you never been in a swimming hole before?"

He arched his perfectly plucked blond eyebrow. "Do I look like the type? Just the word hole implies a bottomless dark pit teeming with slimy underwater...creatures."

The disgusted look on his face made me chuckle. "Like water moccasins and leeches?"

Kelley gasped, winding his arms around my neck. "Say you're kidding me! Get out!"

"Only a little bit, Fancy."

"No, I mean get out! Literally. Out of the water!"

I gave in to the moment and wrapped my arms around his slim waist. "Don't worry, I'll make sure to check your body real good when we get out."

"That *almost* sounds worth getting bitten to experience."

He wrapped his long legs around my waist, and I felt his half-hard dick press against my stomach. He was killing me, weakening my resolve to dust, with his mouth so close to mine and his erection pushing into me just above my own.

It would be too easy to give in to the temptation of his sweet lips. I could still taste them from the mere brush we shared the night before. But where would that leave me? Aching and desperate for a man I had no future with. Just like with Mike.

No, I'd learned my lesson years ago. I wasn't keen to repeat it.

No matter how lush his mouth looked or how long his lashes seemed. I could resist him. I had to. It was a matter of self-preservation.

"I think it's about time we got out of the water and warmed up."

"Is that an invitation?"

My mouth twisted, and I hoped the look I gave him made it clear I wasn't playing games. He hopped down from my arms and the space against my chest was replaced with cold water, effectively dousing any residual heat I might have felt from his suggestion. I climbed out of the spring, and he followed, going straight for the towels I'd laid over the hood of the truck to warm in the sun.

"You hungry?"

"I guess I could eat."

"There's a good barbecue place not far from here. It's not much to look at, but you'll never forget the food. They serve a mile high barbecue brisket sandwich that you would swear was made by God himself." Kelley didn't look impressed, and I chuckled. "They also serve a Cobb salad that Carlisle swears is the best he's ever had."

"That definitely seems much more to my liking." Kelley pulled on a pair of gray sweatpants and a cropped hot pink sweatshirt. "Will they serve me like this?"

"I know the stereotype you must have about these backwater mountain people, but I promise you, the man that runs the barbecue place is accepting. I've known him for years." When we were dried off and buckled into our seats in the truck, I met his eyes across the center console. "Do you really think I'd take you somewhere that would make you feel uncomfortable or unwanted? You should know me better than that by now."

He laid his hand on my arm, his red nails a bright contrast against my tan skin. "I do. I was just worried I would embarrass you."

Something akin to heartburn gripped my chest every time he spoke like that. "That's not possible. Don't ever say anything like that again. Any man would feel proud to have you on his arm. And anyone who doesn't, doesn't deserve a minute of your time."

His comment bothered me as I drove to the restaurant. How many men had made him second guess himself? The thought made me irrationally angry. Kelley was a bright rainbow with a big, soft heart of gold. He shone brighter than anyone I'd ever met, and to think that someone would ask him to dim that light in order to feel more comfortable with themself was unfathomable. I could just imagine some schmuck he met at the bar or at one of his other performances, asking him to remove his nail polish before he met their friends, or asking him to wipe his lipstick off before they entered a restaurant. It made me feel more protective of him than ever, and not just to keep him safe from his stalker, but to protect him from anyone who couldn't appreciate how perfect he was.

I would never ask him to change who he was, the very core of him that made him sparkle like a bright diamond, to suit myself or someone else. Fuck them. Fuck all of them!

As it turned out, taking a burlesque dancer to a barbecue joint was enough to put a smile on my face the rest of the day.

The look of pure unadulterated horror on his handsome face as I stretched my lips around the thick brisket sandwich, dripping with juice down into my beard, made me laugh, which caused me to choke. I dropped the sandwich on my plate and coughed into my napkin, trying to clear my throat.

"You wanna try one of my pickled onions?"

"Is that what we're calling it now? I give you credit for coming up with something original I haven't heard before." His smile was pure sass. He really enjoyed teasing me. The banter felt like another form of foreplay. It was friendly, but also made me think wicked thoughts about him. "I'll never understand you Southerners and your addiction to fried and pickled foods. I mean, you'll literally pickle anything. Pig's feet, bull testicles, you name it."

My laugh was loud enough to draw attention from other customers. "I might have a jar of pickled sausages back at the cabin."

Kelley waved his manicured hand. "Of course you do. Doesn't surprise me at all. Just don't expect me to eat one. And please, for the love of God, don't eat one in front of me."

"What? You don't want to see me slurp some sausage into my mouth?"

He narrowed his beautiful blue eyes. "I would, if you were seriously flirting with me. But since you're just teasing to get a reaction out of me, I'm going to ignore that."

AFTER ANOTHER NIGHT outdoors by the fire pit, we settled on the couch to watch one of the classic movies I had in my vast VHS collection. I couldn't recall how many countless nights I'd sat on this couch and watched this movie, or one just like it, in silence. All by myself. And I'd thought I had it made. But that memory didn't hold a candle to what I felt now. The movie was one Kelley had never seen, and his reactions made it all the more interesting to me, as if I were watching it again for the first time. We shared a bowl of microwave popcorn, and I couldn't remember the last time I enjoyed a movie so much.

It had nothing to do with Kevin Costner, and everything to do with Kelley Michaelson.

Everything was just better and brighter—more memorable—with him by my side.

I'm so fucked.

The rational part of my brain could try to convince me all it wanted not to fall for this man, but the irrational part, which was the part I used most often, wasn't listening. It was happening against my will, whether I wanted to or not.

IT WASN'T long before we were faced with the dilemma of sharing a bed again.

I wrapped the towel around my hips and stared at my reflection in the mirror as I combed my wet hair, the spiky gray ends standing at full salute. After a quick brush of my teeth, I stepped out of the bathroom, followed by a cloud of billowing steam.

"It's all yours."

I moved over to the dresser and grabbed a clean pair of briefs and a T-shirt as Kelley stepped around me to get in the bathroom.

I didn't miss the way his eyes lingered on the beads of water rolling down my chest. When he closed the door behind him, I climbed into bed, deciding at the last minute not to wear the T-shirt. I never slept in one at home. If he liked to look at my chest, who was I to stop him? I smiled to myself as I heard him singing in the shower, some pop song from a boy band that topped the charts recently. It was impossible not to imagine his incredible body naked under the spray of hot water as he soaped it with a sudsy sponge. What I wouldn't give to be that sponge. Or loofah, as Kelley called it.

When he stepped from the bathroom twenty minutes later wearing teeny tiny purple satin shorts and a matching camisole top, I second-guessed my decision to sleep in nothing but my underwear. He was enough temptation for twenty men, and I was only one man.

It was going to be a long night.

His shorts were so tiny and loose that when he climbed into bed, I glimpsed the tip of his soft dick dangling out the side of the leg hole. Which is when I realized he wasn't wearing panties underneath. In fact, he wasn't wearing *anything*. And if tonight went anything like last night had, he would be snuggling that tight ass right up against my body.

Fuck me.

We started out on the right track, with several inches between us, but it wasn't long before he began to shift and scoot in my direction. The entire process took almost twenty minutes of subtly worming his way into my embrace. I almost wished he'd just scoot all the way the fuck over at once and end the charade so I could relax. With a deep sigh of defeat, I allowed him to grab my hand and place it on his thigh, his very smooth and very bare thigh.

"That's better," he surmised, worming deeper into my arms.

"You're like a toddler. You don't give up until you get your way."

He giggled quietly, and I smiled at the sweet sound. "It really is just easier to give me what I want."

I swallowed hard. "And what is it that you want?"

"More of this," he said, emphasizing his words by bumping his ass into my crotch.

"This?" I questioned.

"It feels really good when you hold me like this and put your arms around me. You generate more heat than an electric blanket, and you smell fantastic. Is that old spice soap?"

I laughed because he'd hit the nail right on the head. "Is it a favorite of yours?"

"It is now," he answered softly.

Fuck, he was killing me, and not just from the build up of unreleased hormones. His heart was killing mine. More like owning it, carving out a chunk of it for himself, and I was afraid I wouldn't get it back. Would the hole he left last another two decades like the last one had? With a deep breath, I tried to relax my muscles and settle into his warmth. He smelled like apples and cinnamon, and I struggled not to bury my face in his silky blond hair.

"When we go back home, we can't do this anymore," I whispered.

"I knew you were going to say something like that.

I'm really not interested in listening to any of your self-imposed rules and excuses."

God, he was stubborn. "Kelley—"

"Shh. Just be quiet and let me enjoy one more night of this while I can. Good night, Graham."

"Good night, Fancy."

Just one more night. I was afraid to close my eyes for fear it would be over too soon.

10

KELLEY

THE PEACEFUL SERENITY of the mountain soothed something inside of me, deep down in my soul, in the void created by parents who couldn't accept me and a society that, for the most part, didn't understand me. The natural rugged beauty, untouched by civilization and technology, was an escape that calmed my wild spirit better than yoga or meditation could. I already missed it and I hadn't even left yet. The cabin was swimming holes and fire pits, star-gazing and bird-watching, trout fishing and fresh clean pine-scented air. It felt like home. A home I'd never experienced before, but instantly bonded with. Funny how wherever Graham was, that feeling followed him.

As if on cue, Graham pushed through the screen door, carrying two frosty cold glasses of sweet tea. He handed one to me, brushing his fingertips over mine as I accepted the glass.

"What are you thinking about?"

"How much I'm going to miss this place."

"We can stay a few more days if you want," he suggested, taking a seat in the rocking chair next to mine. The old, weathered wood creaked under his weight.

I smiled softly. "It's time to go home. We both have jobs to return to. I can't hide forever."

His expression turned fierce. "You can hide as long as you need to."

The brand-new feelings that had developed for him over the last few days solidified a little more, suffusing my heart with warmth. "Have I told you how much stronger I feel just by knowing you're in my corner?"

Graham swallowed, and I tracked the movement as his throat moved. "That feels good to hear."

He looked like he wanted to say more but couldn't find the words. "I'm ready. To go home and face whatever comes my way. And I know you'll be right behind me to catch me if I fall." I reached out to touch his thigh. "I needed this break. It was good for me. A chance to clear my head and take a deep breath."

"I'm glad I gave that to you." He covered my hand with his. "You are welcome here anytime you need to breathe, with or without me."

I WATCHED the pine trees fly by my window in a sixty-mile-an-hour blur, feeling sadder with each passing mile that separated me from Rook Mountain. But with each mile closer to Cooper's Cove, I felt more resolute. I could be as strong as Graham believed me to be. I'd buckle down and focus harder on my goals.

"Have you figured out what you want to do with your apartment?"

"I can't ever go back there. He was in my space, touching my things. It's tainted now. Even if they catch him, I'll always see him in every shadow, waiting to jump around every corner and get me."

"So we'll pack up your things and move everything you have into my home."

He made it sound like the easiest thing in the world. "It's not that simple."

"Of course it is. Unless you're referring to the ridiculous amount of things you own."

"Graham—"

He took his eyes off the road to glare at me. "Don't start."

"It's just that I feel like—"

"I know how you feel. But do I honestly make you feel that way?" I shook my head. "That's *your* baggage. Leave it at the door when you move into my home."

Trying to change his mind was like trying to move a brick wall. "Fine," I huffed. "But only if you let me contribute."

Graham scoffed like I said something funny. "Contribute to what?"

"The bills. Utilities, groceries, the mortgage."

"Kelley, get real. I've lived alone my entire life. Paying bills is nothing for me. It's not a hardship. Use this time to save your money until you figure out what you wanna do next."

If only I had a clue what that was. My head and my heart were stuck somewhere between my future independence and wanting that future to somehow include Graham.

WHEN WE RETURNED to the house, I spent the remainder of the afternoon doing laundry. We decided to do something easy for dinner, takeout from the Greek place down the street, and after watching a movie together, decided to call it an early night. I had so much on my mind that I found it difficult to fall asleep easily. I kept replaying our conversation about me moving in permanently, and how Graham wouldn't let me contribute to the bills. It was funny how all of my previous arguments about independence didn't even cross my mind. The thought that weighed most heavily was that I didn't want Graham to think or feel as if I were using him as a human credit card. I didn't see him as a sugar daddy. I saw him as a man who had so many outstanding qualities that his age never factored into the equation.

He was sexy and fun, smart and brave, and so loving and loyal. His list of attributes went on and on. The more I thought about his offer, the more I wanted it, wanted to stay with him, but not so I could figure out my next move.

I wanted to stay with Graham so I could build a life with him.

After that thought became crystal clear in my mind, I was able to fall asleep easily. I woke up the next morning feeling totally refreshed. I set my purple mat on the floor in front of the enormous windows in the living room and placed my phone on the tripod that sat on the coffee table. It was the perfect height to catch my entire body in the frame from my position on the floor. As I began to stretch, the tightness in my muscles loosening like a flag unfurling in the wind, I greeted my followers. I always started out my videos by explaining that yoga was for everyone if you tailored it to your needs and limitations. After another three minutes of stretching, I folded my body into a camel pose and sat up on my knees as I bent my body in a backward arch to touch my toes. Graham shuffled by, heading straight to the kitchen in search of coffee. Usually, when he heard me talking to myself, he knew I was filming and remained quiet. But it was hard not to notice him when he walked around shirtless, his cock making a thick outline in his thin cotton sleep pants, still heavy from the remnants of his morning wood.

I watched him in my peripheral vision as I ran through my routine, ending with a five-minute guided meditation and deep breathing exercise. As soon as I turned off the camera, Graham said, "Good morning, sunshine."

Unfolding myself from the mat, I stood and stretched, bending at the waist to touch my toes before planting my palms flat on the floor and walking my hands out several inches in front of me. The stretch felt incredible on my back, while also making my backside look incredible. A quick peek behind me showed Graham was definitely checking out my ass, and I smiled, feeling ten feet tall from his attention.

"Good morning to you, too. I have one more video to

make in the kitchen as I prepare my green shake. Would you like me to make you one?"

"God, no." He cringed, looking as if I had offered him the blood and guts of cockroaches.

I laughed, and the sound brought a smile to his face, which made me glow brighter than the morning sun shining through the windows. "How about I fix you something delicious? No greens," I promised, winking at him as I grabbed my phone and bounced into the kitchen.

I set the tripod on the counter across from me and stood behind the kitchen island, measuring out the ingredients for my shake. Whey and protein powders, dehydrated kelp, carrots and spinach, mango juice and orange juice, and a shot of liquid vitamins.

As I talked into the camera, I heard the rustling of Graham's newspaper in the background and smiled inwardly. I loved everything about living here. His routine had become so familiar to me, and I craved it. Compared to my studio apartment, where my life had felt small and lonely, this home felt like I'd opened all the curtains on the windows and let the sunshine into my life. All the little things about cohabitating with someone brought me comfort and joy. And when I stopped to consider it, I realized I never wanted to leave. Never wanted to leave *him*.

His classic rock music that drifted in from the garage when he worked on his bike. The sound of the lawnmower early Sunday morning as he cut the grass while I peeked at his shirtless sweaty body through the window like a voyeur. The smell of bleach and other chemicals that clung to his hands after he cleaned the pool. His cologne, spicy yet musky, ignited my pheromones and made me want to have his babies. When he ducked out to the convenience store or the gas station and never failed to ask me if I needed or wanted something. Graham was a wonderful partner, so easy to live with. He deferred to me in the kitchen without expecting it of me. Always thanked me for the littlest things I did for him. As opposite as we were, our personalities meshed seamlessly. And it was all of these little things, a thousand countless ways that filled my soul with purpose and joy, that eased the feeling of loneliness I had felt for so long while living alone. I never wanted to go back to that life again.

After giving my shake the final taste test and telling my viewers how delicious it was, I switched off the camera and began making Graham's shake. Turmeric and nutmeg to reduce inflammation in his joints, ginger and powdered garlic for his immune system and heart health, fish oil and omega three liquid vitamins for brain health and lower cholesterol, a banana for potassium, and a mango for taste. I dipped a straw into the drink and brought both his and mine into the living room.

"Thank you. You didn't have to do that for me," he insisted, and I got the feeling it was less of a compliment and more of an actual truth. He really didn't want to taste what I'd concocted for him.

Graham raised the straw to his lips, and I smiled, anticipating his reaction. He choked, predictably, smacking himself in the chest as he forced himself to swallow it down his throat.

"It's an acquired taste," I joked, taking a large sip of my own shake.

"Clearly," he agreed, coughing. "But I'm going to drink every last drop." He smiled and took another sip without gagging while he continued to stare at me.

"What?" I asked, unable to read him. He looked amused or satisfied. I really couldn't tell which.

"No one has ever tried to manage me before. It's kind of nice."

He liked my managing ways.

His praise made me positively glow. We were on the right path, even if he didn't realize it. Back at the cabin, I'd made up my mind about Graham Carrick, and when I set my mind on something, I followed through to the very end. I was determined to prove to him how much he needed me, how indispensable I could be to him, and just how much happiness and pleasure I could bring to his life. He seemed like a tough nut to crack, but I had a few tricks up my sleeve. I also suspected he had a gooey center inside that hard shell, and I couldn't wait to lick him like the sweetest dessert.

AFTER HAVING BEEN GONE for several days, our refrigerator was empty. Graham and I made a quick run to the grocery store, and I decided to make vegetable fajitas for dinner. It was the perfect excuse to wear the white cotton blouse embroidered with colorful flowers that reminded me of something I would find in a Mexican street market. I paired it with extremely short denim shortalls and a purple headband that sported a large bow. I thought it was a festive and fun look. When

Graham laid his eyes on me, he chuckled with amusement, but I could see a touch of fondness in his smile that reached his eyes. As outrageous as my style seemed to him, I knew he loved it.

In my experience, men loved the satin and silk, the leather and lace, that I wore during my performances, but this ultra-femme cuteness? Not so much. Especially not on a big, muscled body like mine. But knowing how much Graham liked it made me look forward to getting dressed, to his reaction. I found myself dressing for him, wanting to choose something that would bring him pleasure and make him look at me with that fond little smile that made me feel almost giddy.

"What smells so amazing?"

I stirred the strips of cut vegetables in the frying pan, sending a fragrant cloud of steam wafting into my face and scenting the air with the smell of cumin and chipotle seasonings. "Vegetable fajitas."

"Mmm, that must be why you're dressed for Cinco De Mayo."

Laughing, I smacked him playfully with the oven mitt before bending over the oven to remove a tray of warm flour tortillas. At the same moment, Graham tried to move around me, and we danced awkwardly around each other. When I moved right, so did he. I went left, and he followed.

"Stop moving," he growled, gripping my hips to keep me still.

I placed my mitted hands around his waist, not actually able to grab onto him through the thick padding, just needing to reach out to him in some way. Graham took a step closer to me and dragged his nose along my neck.

"You smell like watermelon." His deep gravelly voice made my pulse skyrocket. He inhaled deeply and sighed, and every tight place inside of me loosened and opened for him. My body, my heart, everything. God how I wanted to belong to this man, wanted him to claim me, take me, touch and taste me. Even if only for a handful of hours at most.

I closed my eyes and tipped my head back, exposing my throat to him. The brush of his lips across my skin made heat gather in my belly. Graham raised his head, and I sensed he was looking at me. I blinked my eyes open to see his bright green irises burning into mine as he cupped the back of my neck. His thumb stroked lazily, possessively, over the pulse in my throat that fluttered wildly under his touch. I swallowed hard, making my Adam's apple bob under his thumb. He pressed against it slightly, and my gut swirled with anticipation and lust. It was a struggle to breathe because of the tangle of nerves gathered in my chest, blocking my airway. He bent his head, bringing his lips within an inch of mine. I could feel his breath, swallow it into my mouth as he continued to linger, drawing out the moment when he brushed his lips over mine. Molten lava flowed through my veins, thick and hot, making my body burn up and my brain sluggish. My entire world was reduced to his mouth, waiting to taste him, to feel him connect with mine.

"Kelley," he breathed over my lips.

His grip on my throat tightened as his mouth touched mine, his tongue becoming one with mine as they slid together. I groaned into the kiss, my body melting into him, sagging against his chest as he supported my weight. Graham was voracious, kissing me with a hungry urgency, like he was starved for me. I couldn't breathe, couldn't think, my body on autopilot, driven by my need for him. He sucked on my tongue in hard pulls, drawing it into his mouth, stroking it. I felt it all the way to my toes, like pinpricks of electricity shooting through my limbs. There wasn't a single part of my body that wasn't fully invested in the kiss.

The sound of a key in the door echoed in the silence, making him jump back, and I groaned miserably. "Shannon," he rasped, sounding almost pained.

I stood there, frozen, my brain disoriented and numb. Graham squeezed my hip before letting me go.

"I'm sorry," he whispered. I wondered if he was apologizing for kissing me or being interrupted.

I shook my head to clear the fog. "Oh, I'll just...step aside and collect myself. Freshen up." I fled the kitchen just as his son walked through the front door.

His deep voice carried down the hall. "Hey, Pops! I smell dinner. You didn't happen to save me any, did you?"

I could hear every word exchanged between them through the thin door of the bedroom.

"Shannon, I love you like a son, but I swear to God, someone better have died."

I smothered my laughter as I sagged against the door, in complete agreement with him. I fanned my overheated and flushed skin with my hand and then ran to look in the mirror over my dresser to see if his fingers had left marks on my neck. Sadly, they hadn't, and I felt mildly disappointed.

Out in the living room, Shannon laughed. "Where's Kelley?"

"In the bedroom."

"Oh, yeah? Whose?"

I heard Graham growl like a feral animal. "I swear to God, if someone isn't dead, they are about to be."

"Who, me?"

He sounded like he was enjoying giving his father a hard time. Graham had to feel as shaken as I did. He needed rescuing.

"Most likely," he warned. "Tell me you have a great reason for being here."

"Can't I just come and visit my old man?"

"Shannon..."

He laughed, thoroughly amused. I walked out of the bedroom, pretending as if I hadn't heard him arrive.

"Oh, hi, Shannon. Nice of you to visit."

"No, it's not," Graham insisted.

"Actually, I do have a reason for stopping by."

"Then fucking get to it," he grated, crossing his thick arms over his chest.

"Two actually." Shannon turned to me, a huge grin on his handsome face. "Kelley, my entertainment for tomorrow night canceled on me last minute. I'd rather have you perform twice in one week than have an empty stage. You interested?"

I brightened instantly. "Yes, definitely. Thank you for thinking of me."

"Fantastic. What's the second thing?"

I tried to cover my smile. He was out of patience with his son and desperate to shove him out the door.

"Carson and Ryan are getting married."

"I know. I was there. Did you forget I was the one shoving a phone in their face to take pictures?"

Shannon laughed. "I know. What I meant was, we need to discuss our plans to celebrate. We're going to throw them a big engagement party here, by the pool."

"Of course we are. I'll get right on it. Anything else?"

"Nope," he said, rocking on his heels as his gaze volleyed back and forth between us. "Just wanted to stop by and deliver the news in person."

"How thoughtful of you," Graham said with a touch of sarcasm. "Couldn't you have just called?"

"I could have, but this is way more fun," he said with an unrepentant grin.

Despite my irritation, I smiled along with Shannon. He was a hoot. Graham, however, wasn't smiling.

"Well, it's late and we're about to sit down to dinner, so it's time for you to head back to wherever it is you came from. Thanks for stopping by."

"Pops, you can't be serious. You aren't gonna invite me to stay for dinner?" Shannon's face lost all traces of humor.

"Of course he's not serious. I'll set an extra place for you," I said, admonishing Graham with my eyes.

Graham's obvious annoyance at Shannon made Shannon chuckle. I was going to have my hands full with those two during dinner.

11

GRAHAM

"GRAHAM," Kelley called out from somewhere in the house. His voice carried into my bedroom. "Have you seen my black satin glove?"

Fuck.

Oh, I had seen it, all right, when I had worn it while jacking off to his video. How was I going to dig my way out of this?

I grabbed his glove from my nightstand drawer and tucked it into my back pocket. Just as I reached the living room, so did Kelley. He was dressed in a strapless, black velvet sheath gown that hugged him tight everywhere. The damn thing looked painted onto his body. Black silk stockings and stilettos peeped from the slit in the gown that reached from his ankle to his thigh, showing a tantalizing glimpse of the lace band that topped the thigh-high stocking, and the garter belt attached to it. His make up was dramatic, smoky eyes and scarlet lips. The rosy blush accented his perfectly chiseled cheekbones.

My dick immediately hardened in my jeans. My

fingers itched to touch the velvet that covered his hips and ample ass. He must have tucked and taped his dick, because I couldn't detect a bulge under his dress. How was that comfortable? How did he move so gracefully across the stage with his generous-sized cock tucked between his legs? And I knew it was generously sized, because I'd seen the man in a skimpy bikini more than once. I guessed like with anything, practice made perfect.

"Oh, there you are," he said with a breezy laugh. "I'm looking for my black satin glove. I was only able to find one. Have you seen it?"

It was difficult to swallow past the lump of nerves forming in my throat, as I reached into my back pocket and produced his glove. Despite the years of poker I played, my face was going to give me away any moment.

"How convenient," he said, with a sly look. Kelley brought the glove to his nose and sniffed it while his eyes remained locked with mine. "It smells like fabric softener. Did you wash it?"

Beads of sweat gathered in the pits of my arms. But instead of spewing lies, I chose to remain silent. Which probably said more than it didn't. Kelley was able to read between the lines like a pro.

His beautiful blue eyes twinkled mischievously. "That must mean it got dirty. I wonder how that could have happened. Any ideas?" He arched his blond eyebrow, awaiting my answer.

Yeah, I had nothing. I was screwed and he knew why.

I was proud of myself for continuing to maintain eye contact with him, while appearing outwardly calm, cool, and collected.

Slowly, Kelley slid the glove over his fingers and up his arm, making a sensual show of it. "Thank you for washing it for me. It's a shame it's just going to get dirty again tonight." He gave me a pointed look. "After the show, that is." Then he turned on his razor-sharp heel and sashayed down the hall, calling out over his shoulder in a nonchalant voice, "Let me know if you ever need to borrow it again. We can share it."

I palmed my face, completely humiliated. Damn, that man was a flirt, and he had my number. I hadn't fooled him for a second. And yet, the humiliation didn't sting so bad seeing how excited Kelley seemed by the idea I had used his glove as a cum-rag. It was becoming increasingly clear to me just how much he wanted my attention. Which was convenient because I was finding it more difficult with each passing day, each flirty wink and air kiss he blew in my direction, to ignore my attraction to him.

WE ARRIVED at Limericks thirty minutes before Kelley was due on stage, which gave him just enough time to chug a bottle of water and stretch. How the man accomplished a warm up in four-inch heels and a painted-on dress, I'll never know. It was fucking impressive.

I stepped behind the bar to catch up with Shannon.

"Hey, Pops. I texted you the details of the engagement party. If you need me to come by the house this week before work and help you clean up the back yard, let me know."

"I think it's in good shape. I just added chemicals to the pool, so it shouldn't be too strong by Saturday."

His ice-blue eyes twinkled with mischief. "So, are you going to tell me what really happened on your trip to the cabin?"

"Nothing. It was uneventful and relaxing."

Shannon crossed his thick tatted arms over his chest and smiled. "What a shame."

"Would you quit that bullshit? Stop trying to make something out of nothing." But it *was* something lately. That fucking kiss that was hot enough to singe the hair on my balls was definitely *something*.

"Hey, Pops? That look on your face says differently." He shoved my arm playfully. "You were always shit at poker, old man."

I was thankful for the interruption when Aries, a friend of ours and talented tattoo artist, sidled up to the bar. "Hey, Graham. Hey, Shannon." He barely spared me a glance, his eyes fixed on my son instead.

"Hey, Aries."

"Hey, Aries. You stop by for a drink?" Shannon asked.

"Nah, I'd rather wait until you make good on your offer to take me out for one." His breezy smile stole some of the boldness from his words. "I just stopped by to grab takeout and talk to Gordy."

Just then, my nephew stepped out of the kitchen carrying a takeout bag.

"Here ya go," he said, offering the bag to Aries.

"Thanks. Have I told you guys how much I love his meatloaf special?"

"I think you mentioned it once or twice," Shannon quipped, chewing on a toothpick. "Nobody makes it as good as Gordo here," he said, clapping his cousin on the back a little too harshly.

"Fuck off," Gordy mumbled, shrugging Shannon off.

"Gordy, you still have that room for rent?"

I eyed my nephew curiously. "I wasn't aware you were looking for a roommate. Last thing you said was how excited you were to finally have the house to yourself."

Shannon added his two cents to stir the pot, as always. "Yeah, Gordo. Thought you loved living alone."

Gordy glared at him before giving Aries his attention. "Yeah, I still got that room, if you want it."

"It's closer to my shop than my current place, and the rent is cheaper. Of course I want it. Plus, I'd get to hang out with you more, since you always seem too busy for me lately. The only time I see you anymore is when I have you in my chair in the shop."

"Gordo, just think of all the meatloaf you could make for your buddy," Shannon teased.

"I'll call you tonight on my break," Gordy promised. Then, with one last glare at Shannon, he returned to the kitchen.

"You still owe me that drink, Shannon. Soon," Aries warned before he grabbed his food from the counter and left.

"What in the fuck was that all about? And since when the fuck do we serve a meatloaf special?"

I didn't understand Shannon's deep belly laugh.

"Since Aries says it's his favorite. I don't think he realizes it's not on the menu."

"Jesus, what a mess. And now he's gonna move in with Gordy? Does he have any idea Gordy likes him?"

Shannon smiled, shaking his head. "I'm not convinced Gordy knows either." His smile widened more. The rivalry between my son and nephew ran deep and long, and Shannon loved to fan the flames of discord between them whenever he could.

"Stay out of it, Shannon," I warned. "Gordy's a big boy. Let him handle it on his own."

"He sure is a big boy," he joked.

"Knock it off." I tossed a bar rag at him. "I'm going to see if Kelley is done warming up and ready to take the stage." With a last look at him, I warned, "Behave yourself."

"You first, Pops." He chuckled, and I rolled my eyes, wishing I could wring his neck every once in a while.

I found him in the narrow hall behind the stage, smoothing his perfectly gelled and styled hair. "You've never looked fancier, Fancy. You about ready?"

"Yes. I'm sufficiently warmed up, loose, and hydrated. Are you going to watch the show?"

I met his stare directly. "I wouldn't miss it."

Kelley was scheduled to dance for four songs, and when he took the stage, the lights dimmed and the large crowd gathered in the lounge hushed. Purple and blue lights shined down on him, highlighting his stunning good looks. Several guests gasped when they saw his gown. He looked absolutely stunning.

He warmed up his audience with an old Tina Turner song, working his way across the stage with a sexy slink of his velvet-sheathed hips. Kelley had mastered the art of movement. He could seduce a crowd of people with the way he walked. I watched, mesmerized, as his hands moved down his chest and abs, over the softness of his dress and the hardness of his body. Satin gloves whispered over black velvet, teasing the onlookers as he stroked over his hips and ass, down his thighs, tracing the slit in his gown.

During the second song, he unzipped his gown, the zipper hidden in a seam along the side of his dress, and slunk out of it, letting the fabric pool at his feet. He stepped out of it and kicked it aside, and a collective gasp was heard among the crowd as they saw what he'd worn underneath.

The sheer lace teddy was of the darkest purple, almost black, and hid nothing from the eyes of his audience. Multiple straps criss-crossed his broad back and shoulders, and delicate silver chains draped his hips. When he stepped into the spotlight, I could see his rosy nipples peeking through the lace. When he turned around, I realized it was a thong that rode the crack in his ass cheeks like a tightrope. Jesus H, my mouth watered. A rush of possessiveness overshadowed my common sense, making me want to cover him with my body from prying hungry eyes.

No wonder he'd acquired a stalker. Who could resist this man?

His third number was a series of coordinated gymnastic moves including splits, flips, lunges, and twirls.

How did he not stumble and fall in those mile-high heels? God, he was so talented. The more I watched him, the more I appreciated the extensive training and hard work he put into his craft. He was a master.

For his last performance, he delivered leg kicks that put the Rockettes to shame, more splits, and a floor routine on his knees. He ended the show with the most provocative dance moves that ignited my blood, and the entire time, his eyes had remained fixed on me, as if he were performing only for me. I dreamed of being the only man in the room, and having the guts to show him just how much he affected me when he danced.

Fuck, the man affected me when he smiled, when he talked—when he fucking breathed.

If I was going to stand a chance of surviving living with him, I would need to somehow separate the man he was on stage from the man he was at home. Which was next to impossible considering he was just as sexy at home, usually choosing to underdress in bikinis and workout gear more often than actual clothes.

The music tapered off, and the lights dimmed. Kelley waved goodbye to roaring applause. I ducked through the side door next to the stage that led to the hallway in back just as Kelley popped through the curtain, making his way down the hall to me holding his discarded gown. His duffel bag sat on the floor, halfway between us, and when we neared, we both froze, staring at it. A single red rose lay on top of the zippered bag.

"Motherfucker."

Kelley swallowed, looking apprehensive before he kneeled in front of the bag.

"Don't touch it. God knows what he did to that bag," I cautioned.

Ignoring me, he grabbed the rose, snapped the thornless stem in half, and threw it down the hallway, yelling, "My favorite color roses are purple, you sick fuck!"

"Don't open the bag, Kelley."

"I need to see inside the bag, Graham. Right now."

"We should call Detective Vallejo." Again, he ignored me, reaching for the zipper, and I yanked the bag from his grasp. "Fine! Let me do it, then."

Slowly, I opened the bag, half expecting a snake to jump out and bite me or something just as macabre. But what I found instead was worse than a reptile. Kelley gasped, peering over my shoulder. His bright pink dildo sat on top of his sweatsuit. It was covered in a sticky substance, and there was a folded note lying next to it. Hesitantly, I reached for the note.

You catch more flies with honey than vinegar. Maybe I haven't been sweet enough to you. I promise to try harder. I will make you mine, Kelley Masters!

P.S. See you real soon, sweet thing.

HE HADN'T SIGNED his name, but he didn't need to. It was obvious who left the note. *Kelley fucking Masters!*

My vision burned bright red with anger, and I struggled to remain calm. But only for his sake. I dropped the note like it burned me and stood, taking Kelley in my arms. His outrage had been replaced by either exhaustion or defeat because tears pooled in his eyes like glittering crystals, spilling down his cheeks in a hot rush.

I shrugged out of my jacket and wrapped the black leather around his shoulders, zipping the front closed before taking him in my arms again. For a minute, he held onto me tightly, crying onto my shoulder, his tears soaking into the cotton T-shirt I wore.

My hand swept up and down his back. "Shh," I whispered. "He doesn't deserve your tears." Kelley lifted his tear-stained face from my shoulder and nodded, swallowing repeatedly as he tried to get himself under control. I held his chin in the palm of my hand and gazed into his kohl-smudged eyes. "Can you be strong for me for a few more minutes until I can get you out of here?"

"Yes, I'm trying. Just take me home, please."

I wanted nothing more, but I had to call this in to detective Vallejo, and wait here for her. Kelley, however, could be interviewed later. I was getting him the fuck out of here. ASAP.

"I don't want you to touch anything in this bag. Just put your dress back on so your bottom half is covered. I'm going to ask Carson or Ryan to drive you home and sit with you until I get there."

"What? Why can't you come with me?"

He sounded close to panic, and I feared he was going to fall apart on me before I could get him out of here. His system was over-flooded with adrenaline and fear and anger, and probably ten other emotions.

"Because, Fancy. I've got to stay here and talk with the detective. I'll be there as soon as I can. I promise." I pressed a kiss to his cheek and released my hold on his chin. The kiss seemed to momentarily confuse him, which was a good thing. I helped him step into the dress, and he slid it up to his waist, letting the bodice sag around his hips. He hooked his arm through mine, and I escorted him down the hall, past the storeroom and the bathroom, past the kitchen, and out to the main bar area. Shannon was behind the counter, serving drinks, and Carson was running them to waiting tables. I caught Carson's gaze and motioned for him to meet me at the bar.

"What's up, Uncle G? By the way, you were amazing, Kelley."

"Thank you," he said, sounding anguished.

"Listen, he was here. Steven Masters."

"His stalker?"

"Yes. He was here."

"When? Where?" he questioned, his eyes darting wildly around the room.

"He's probably long gone, but he left a note and... other things on Kelley's duffel bag in the hall behind the stage during his performance."

Carson's green eyes widened. "I didn't see anyone or notice anything."

"I know, it's okay. I just need you or Ryan to take Kelley home immediately. I have to wait for the detective."

"Sure, of course. Whatever you need. Are you okay, Kelley?"

He nodded meekly and allowed Carson to shower him with concern as he walked him to the bar and sat him on an empty stool.

"Ryan came to see your show. He's still in the lounge. I'll grab him."

Carson dashed into the lounge to look for Ryan. Kelley watched me from across the bar as I pulled my phone out of my back pocket and dialed the detective's number. I gave him a reassuring smile. Detective Vallejo answered on the third ring, and I relayed the whole story. She assured me she was on her way, and I hung up just as Ryan and Carson were escorting Kelley out the door. I quickly caught up with them and pulled Carson aside.

"Go straight home. Lock the doors and set the alarm system. If you hear anything, I don't care if it's the neighbors fucking dog barking, I want you to call the police. Do you understand me?"

"Yes, Uncle G. I'll keep him safe until you get there. You can count on me."

"I know I can. You've never let me down when it counts." I squeezed him to my chest in a quick hug.

ANOTHER HOUR PASSED before I was able to get the fuck out of there and head home to Kelley. He was asleep on the couch when I came in, curled into Ryan's side with his knees tucked up under him. They were beautiful together; two blond heads, two pairs of pretty blue eyes, and two soft hearts that shone pure as gold.

"How is he?"

"I think his adrenaline spike crashed. He fell asleep in the middle of his sentence."

"Thank you for sitting with him."

Carson clapped me on the shoulder. "I was happy to do it. I hate that you're going through this. I know how much you care about him. I mean, we all do. Kelley is a great guy. Ryan is crazy about him. But I know you're taking this extra hard because you feel responsible for him. I'm here if you need anything, and if this weekend isn't a good time—"

"No. This asshole isn't going to delay our family celebration. Kelley is beyond excited for you and Ryan. He would be crushed if we had to cancel because of him. It'll be good for him. He needs the distraction and the company."

I thanked Ryan for looking after Kelley and locked the door behind them on their way out. Kelley hadn't moved when Ryan disentangled himself. He was still asleep, curled in a ball and wearing my jacket. There was no way I could lift him, he was nearly the same size as me, but I hated to leave him on the couch alone. Instead, I sat down next to him and slid my arm around his back. Immediately, he snuggled close and laid his head on my chest.

"You're back," he murmured.

"I promised I would be. Why don't you let me help you to bed?"

"I'd rather stay here. With you." He raised his half-lidded sleepy eyes to me. "Will you stay with me?"

"Fuck." Like I could deny him anything. "Can we at

least go and lay down? I don't think my back can take this couch all night."

I followed him into my bedroom, feeling all kinds of nervous and uncomfortable as he unzipped my borrowed jacket and shrugged out of it, revealing the sheer purple lace bodysuit he performed in earlier. Then he slid the velvet dress down his legs, along with the stockings, and climbed into bed from the foot of it, crawling over the length of the mattress to reach the pillows, the thong separating his firm cheeks on full display.

Goddamn, but I was a glutton for punishment.

Somehow, I was supposed to sleep next to him all night and not think about my dick.

"Did you want to shower or change into something...more?"

"More?" He settled his head on the pillow and sighed.

"Something with more material."

He chuckled and patted the empty space beside him. *My* spot. "All I need is you."

"Kelley—"

"Just come hold me. You said you didn't mind."

"I don't. I just—" Shit. I just what? Want to fuck you? Want to touch you? Want to take you in my arms and never let you go? I laughed without humor. "You're killing me, Fancy. You know that, right?"

Kelley's laugh held a trace of the humor mine lacked. "You'll live."

I peeled my shirt over my head and stepped out of my jeans, rounding the bed to my side, and crawled beneath the cool sheets in just my black briefs.

He eyed my body like a starving man at a buffet. "You wear those so well."

"You aren't supposed to notice stuff like that."

"Why not? I'm not a child, Graham. I'm a sexually active male and you're gorgeous and available. I'd have to be blind not to notice, and even then, I think I would."

"Quit flirting and come here." I pulled him into my arms, and he settled on my chest with his hand lying on my pecs. Kelley yawned and closed his eyes, his warm, soft breaths teasing the hair on my chest. His fingers toyed with my nipple, idly tracing circles around the aureole and flicking the tip.

I ran my fingers through his hair, partly stiff from the gel he used for his performance. "We're gonna get him, Kelley, I promise you."

"I know. I'm not naïve enough to believe I'm out of danger just because you're stuck to me like nipple pasties —" I barked out a laugh, charmed by his analogy, "—but I don't feel scared when I'm with you. Angry, yes, but completely safe."

"*Mostly* safe. Never completely."

He rolled my nipple between his thumb and index finger, causing a delicious burn and shifted his knee over my crotch, discreetly rubbing the thickening bulge. He might have meant to be subtle, but it was a blatant move. I could scold him, or I could shut the fuck up. The latter sounded way more appealing. I was almost curious to see what he would attempt next.

12

KELLEY

I WAS WELL aware I was pushing his limits, but I'd be damned if I planned on stopping. I'd made up my mind to make Graham mine, and I was hell-bent on seducing him—not full-on siren seduction—but something softer, that wouldn't scare him away. Graham was an alpha male, the patriarch of his family, used to taking charge, and he needed to come to this decision on his own.

Or at least, he needed to think he had.

I let my lips, just a hair's breadth away from his nipple, brush over the tight peak. My tongue followed, licking softly at first, and then more boldly.

"You trying to make me lose control?"

His voice sounded rough and deep, a clear sign of how he was feeling. Ignoring him, because it was obvious I was trying to steal his self-control, I sucked the stiff bud between my lips, drawing on it hard enough that he would feel it in his balls.

"Christ!"

He gripped my shoulders, rolled me beneath him,

and gazed down into my eyes, bright with desire and need.

"This what you wanted?" he rasped, his gaze slipping down to my mouth.

"God, yes. Need you," I panted breathlessly.

"Be careful what you ask for, Fancy. I just might give it to you."

And he did. Like a recently released inmate unleashing years, decades, of pent-up lust. I was built sturdy, and I hoped he fucking wrecked me.

Graham seized my lips roughly, absolutely devouring them. He bit at my lips, my cheek, his fingers digging into my biceps, the other gripping my jaw hard enough to bruise it. My legs scissored with his, desperately seeking a hold on him. He tugged at my hair, his teeth closing over my earlobe.

"Can't stop. Can't slow down. I gotta have you."

That sounded perfect.

His raw energy drove me wild for him. I was burning up, desperate to be filled. Anywhere. Everywhere.

Graham gripped the thin straps of my bodysuit in his teeth and tore them from my shoulder, ripping the lace and exposing my nipple. He latched on and sucked hard, my back arching off the mattress. I palmed the back of his head, pulling him down to me, imprisoning him.

"You like that?" he growled, going for the other one. He rendered the bodysuit in half, and I gasped. "Don't worry. I'll buy you a new one. In every fucking color."

My eyes drifted to the ceiling, and I smiled, reveling in the moment. He was making love to me. I was finally getting everything I wanted from him, and it was better than I ever could have imagined. He was absolutely primal for me, and I was high on lust and adrenaline, an excess of endorphins coursing through my blood.

Graham's hot mouth trailed wet, sucking kisses down my chest, down my stomach. His tongue traced the dips and valleys of my abs before swirling inside my belly button. I squirmed from the over-sensitized stimulation.

"Dreamed of this," he rasped, his breathing harsh and fast. "Wanted to take my time with you, but I can't." His gaze traveled up the length of my torso, settling on my face. "Gonna tear into you so fucking hard."

My pulse skyrocketed from the delicious threat. Or was it a promise? I hoped it was both.

He worked his way down my body, pulling the torn remnants of lace with him, down over my hips, until my cock was bared, achingly hard and wet at the tip. He groaned as he licked over my slit, tasting me for the first time.

"Goddamn, baby, you taste so fucking sweet."

Graham took my entire length into his mouth, bobbing up and down my shaft with hollowed cheeks. I was so mindless with pleasure I couldn't even remember my own name. His fingers rolled my balls, tugging at them. A spike of pleasure brought me too close to the edge, and I pushed at his head.

"No way," he growled. "Give it to me. Can't wait to swallow your load."

"Ungh!" I cried out, consumed with the need to come. I teetered right on the edge of paradise, so close, yet needing more.

Graham eyed me, his expression savage—fierce. He

poked his tongue deep into my slit, stretching it, and the slight burn made me shoot down his throat. He swallowed every drop and licked his lips with a wicked smile, and then his face disappeared from view as he delved between my cheeks. Again, my back came off the bed, but Graham held my hips down firmly, holding me hostage to the sweet torture his tongue lavished on my hole.

I wanted to taste him. Was dying to feel his thick girth stretch my mouth. I reached for his hips, intending to urge him to roll over, but he snapped at me like an animal. "Don't move!"

"I want to suck you."

He chuckled darkly. "If you touch me, I'll shoot like a rocket and this will all be over. I'm not young like you. Being twenty-four has its benefits." Graham nipped my hip bone lightly with his teeth. "Turn over."

I flipped my body, and he dragged the purple lace down my legs and tossed the ruined garment to the floor. "It's a shame what I did to that. But I like you better like this."

I laughed, agreeing with him. His finger trailed down my crease, and I eagerly anticipated what was coming.

"You want lube, or just spit?"

A laugh cracked from my throat. "What kind of back-alley hookup question is that?"

"What?" he asked, not seeing the problem. Was that what he had become used to in the absence of love?

"Grab the damn lube, please." I hoped the banter gave him a moment to settle. Once I had his dick inside me, I needed him to last as long as possible. I was determined to come on his cock.

Graham smiled and reached beside me in the top drawer of the nightstand, retrieved the bottle, and flipped the cap, drizzling a liberal amount directly over my ass. The cold liquid pooled in my crease, and I shivered as he spread it with his finger, slowly driving me out of my mind. He circled my hole, tapping it lightly, rubbing over it back and forth with the slightest pressure, the tip of his finger dipping deeper with each stroke. I wanted to scream, 'Just do it already'!

"You have the prettiest ass. I could worship it for days," he mused.

"I'll give you three more minutes." I'd reached the limit of my endurance.

Graham chuckled and slid his finger into my passage, moving it in and out with deliberate slowness. "Another one," I barked. He added a second finger, stroking in and out of my heat a little faster, working me up. I bucked my ass, meeting the thrust of his fingers, shoving them deeper inside me to brush over that coveted spot.

Panting and breathless, I begged, "Please, Graham. Fuck me."

"Christ." He sat up and grabbed a condom from the drawer, tearing it open and rolling it over his hard length.

I wondered how he would want to fuck me: on my knees, on my back or stomach, maybe ask me to ride him, but he covered my back with his body and nestled his dick between my cheeks, sliding easily into my slick hole. I tried to crawl to my knees to gain more leverage, but he urged me back down. Graham laced his fingers through mine and stretched my arms above my head, flat against the headboard. He sucked on my neck and collarbone as he fucked into me, deep and slow, adding the weight of his body to the strength of his thrusts. The pleasure was all-consuming and satisfying, the friction of the cotton sheets rubbing on my dick, and in minutes, I was there, spilling onto the bedding beneath me.

"Graham! Fuck, yes. Fuck me."

"Goddamn, Kel." He panted harsh breaths over my neck, beads of sweat dripping from his forehead to land between my shoulder blades, cooling off my heated skin. "Your ass is so fucking tight. You're milking my cock dry."

Yes, I was, because I was strategically squeezing my muscles to make it better for him as he came. He finished, collapsing his weight on my back, pressing me into the mattress. It was a delicious feeling, warm and heavy and secure, and I almost wished he'd fall asleep like this, so I could feel his breath on my skin all night.

All too soon, he rolled off me, planting a kiss between my shoulders, and disappeared into the bathroom. He returned minutes later holding a warm wet cloth and swiped it gently between my legs. With another kiss to each ass cheek, he disappeared again. When he joined me, I scooted over so he could climb under the covers. He reached for me, and I nestled into his furry chest, sighing contentedly. His skin held traces of the tobacco and vanilla cologne I'd come to love so much, and I breathed him in, drifting into a peaceful dream with his scent lingering in my nose.

13

GRAHAM

I WAS the world's biggest fool. It wasn't just sex to me. I was falling hard for him, and when I fell, I did it spectacularly. I offered up my whole heart and soul on a silver platter, along with my undivided attention and unwavering loyalty. Kelley liked me, sure, but he was young, gorgeous, and flirty. So strong and independent. What if his interest in me was only skin-deep and fleeting?

My indecision about how to play this made me grateful for the years I remained single. If I acted like it was nothing but casual sex, he might think I was a callous dickhead. If I chased after him like a bitch in heat, he would think I was a ridiculous Boomer who didn't understand the meaning of friends-with-benefits. What the fuck was I supposed to do?

I stayed up for hours thinking about it while enjoying the sound of his breathing, the warm weight of him in my arms. God, what would it be like to have this every night? *Fucking indescribable.* My eyes became wet, and I hated myself for allowing my heart to want something so badly that it most likely couldn't have.

Why couldn't I ever learn my lesson?

I only managed a few hours of sleep before my eyes blinked open and my mind started whirling again. Carefully, I disentangled myself from him and rolled out of bed. Going commando underneath the sweatpants I grabbed, I padded out to the kitchen on silent feet and prepared the coffee maker. The best game plan I was able to concoct was that I would play it calm and casual, but also, I was making him breakfast. That was more to avoid an awkward morning situation in bed than it was wanting to do something nice for him. Although I did. It was going to be a struggle to keep my hands and mouth off of him today. It would be too easy to fall into him and allow myself to shower him with affection like I wanted to. I was just that kind of sap, the kind that wanted to go out of my way to please him because he made my heart feel like mush.

I was frying up a batch of French toast when I heard him exit the bedroom, and my heart jumped up into my throat. Kelley came into the kitchen wrapped in my black velour robe, his bright red toenails peeking out from beneath the long hem, and wrapped his arms around my waist from behind, snuggling into my back.

"Good morning. Smells delicious."

I swallowed my heart back down into my chest, where it beat a frantic pace. I hadn't prepared myself for this reaction. He was continuing the warm and snugglies, not playing it casual at all.

"Don't get excited, nothing in this pan contains

vegetables."

He peeked over my shoulder at the stove. "French toast? With real maple syrup?" he exclaimed, spying the glass jar on the counter. "Are you trying to destroy my body?"

His voice held a teasing note, but I knew he was more than half serious, not that I could see a damn thing wrong with his body. "Calm down, Fancy. At least I used free-range eggs. That's the best I can offer you."

He smiled and pressed a kiss to my cheek. "I like everything you have to offer me."

What the hell was that supposed to mean? Was he looking for a second round, a repeat of last night? Maybe he wanted to treat it like a honeymoon. A week of banging sex, snuggles, and kisses, before he tired of me.

I served our breakfast at the dining table, which I'd become accustomed to by now. Kelley loved eating there. He went all out at dinner time, with candles and fresh flowers from the backyard.

"What do you have planned for today?"

"I have to teach a dance class at two o'clock, and I was going to hit the gym afterward. What about you?"

"I really need to stop by the bar and check up on it. I haven't been there in over a week. Not since before we left for the cabin."

His eyes sparkled. "Ooh! I haven't been there yet. I'm excited to go with you."

"Well, don't get too excited. I'd hate to disappoint you. It's just a greasy sports bar. You're way too fancy for that place. You'd stick out like a sore thumb."

His beautiful face looked crestfallen, and I realized I

stuck my foot in my mouth, again.

"No bother. I'll just wait in the truck for you while you do your business."

"No, that's not what I meant." I scrubbed my face in frustration and sighed. "What I meant to say was, I wish I had a nicer place to take you. I'm sorry that came out wrong."

"I know you think I'm too fancy for your lifestyle, but I'm just a regular guy, Graham."

I swallowed, feeling ashamed of myself for judging him. He was such a trooper at the cabin, trying his hardest to fit in and enjoy himself. "You're right. And I'm an ass. You know what? I have an idea. Finish your breakfast and get dressed. We have a stop to make on our way to your dance class."

THE SHELTER SMELLED EXACTLY as I remembered it, like bleach and urine. Kelley's face lit up as if I'd driven him to the gates of Disney World.

"Oh my gosh, this is exactly what I needed!" He practically ran through the front doors, making his way to the kitten play area. By the time I caught up with him, he already had his phone out, snapping pictures of the new arrivals. "I'm going to get these uploaded to the shelter's website today." Then, to the kittens, he said, "I better not see you here next time I come," in a voice I assumed was appropriate for kittens, but that I found highly amusing.

I sat in the same chair I occupied last time I came and watched as the kittens surrounded Kelley on the floor. He never complained once about cat hair or razor-sharp kitten claws snagging the threads of his clothes. He was in his element, sunshine and rainbows seeping from his pores as he rolled around with them, handing out cuddles and treats. A woman wearing scrubs decorated with kittens and puppies entered the playroom.

"That's our newest baby," she informed Kelley about the fluffy white kitten he was holding in the crook of his neck. "We haven't named her yet, but since you're here now, why don't you go ahead and do the honors."

You'd think she offered him a winning lottery ticket with the way his face shone with pure joy and excitement. Kelley held the kitten aloft in front of him, staring into her furry little face.

"I think I'll name you Glitter because you shine brighter than all the other kitties. But don't tell them I said that," he added in a loud whisper.

"Glitter is a perfect name for her," the woman agreed. "Now we just need to find her a home."

Some of the light dimmed from Kelley's eyes. "I wish I could take you home with me, baby girl. Someday, when I have my own home, I'll come back for you, and if you're still here, I'll snatch you up and take you home with me."

Fuck me. Fuck me six ways from Sunday. Something like panic gripped my heart just hearing him talk about moving out and finding his own place. That wasn't what I wanted at all. And no matter how many times I invited him to stay, even long-term, Kelley wanted something he could call his own. Someplace where he could hang pictures on the walls and adopt a cat, or twelve.

I wanted to give him that. I wanted my home to be

that place for him. Which meant I was adopting a fucking cat. We were taking Glitter home with us today.

I snuck out of the room while he continued to play and followed the woman up to the registration desk. "Hi, what do I need to do to adopt Glitter?"

"Are you with Kelley?"

"Yeah. I'm a friend of his."

"Well, if the kitten is for him, you don't have to do anything. Kelley has already passed our background check. If he's living in a home that allows pets, he can take Glitter home with him today. It's a thirty-five dollar adoption fee, which I'd be honored to waive because of all that Kelley does here to volunteer. All you need to do is sign the adoption papers and she's yours." She reached into a file cabinet below the desk and pulled out a stack of papers, stapled them together, and handed them to me. "You'll also need to come back in a few weeks when Glitter is old enough to be spayed."

"That's fine. I can do that."

She handed me a pen, and I began to fill out the paperwork. When I got to the line that asked for the adopter's name, I filled out Kelley Michaelson. The woman looked over the paperwork, stamped it, filed it in her drawer, and then handed me an official adoption certificate, hot off the printer.

I was going to need to frame that for him.

I popped my head back into the playroom. "We need to get going if we're gonna make your class in time. I still have one other stop to make." I figured the cat was going to need basic things, like food and litter, so we would need to stop by the pet store on the way to his studio.

With a heavy heart that showed on his face, he said goodbye to Glitter and the rest of the cats.

"Aren't you forgetting something?" I could barely contain my sneaky smile, anticipating the reaction I was about to be blasted with.

Kelley looked around and patted his pockets for his phone. I tipped my head in Glitter's direction. The tiny white kitten sat at his feet, looking up at him with the biggest, roundest green eyes. Almost as big and round as Kelley's. Kelley just looked confused.

"We can't just leave her here. You named her."

Hope bloomed across his face. "You mean...I can take her home with me?"

"Yeah, Fancy. She's yours now. Grab the cat and let's go."

He almost knocked me over when he threw his arms around me, peppering my face with kisses. "Thank you. Thank you. Thank you," he chanted, over and over as he carried the cat to the car.

He settled the kitten in his lap, and I pulled out of the parking lot. "I figured we could stop by the pet store and grab a few basic things we need."

Instead of answering, he sniffled, tears slowly rolling down his cheeks. "I can't believe she's mine. I thought it would be a long, long time before I could ever have a pet of my own. You are the most generous, kind hearted man I've ever known." He shook his head. "I will never be able to repay you for all you've given me."

Whatever he thought I had given him, he'd given me much more. "You don't owe me a damn thing. You have no idea what you give to me. In ways you don't even realize." It became hard to swallow as emotions rushed to the surface. "Just enjoy your cat."

He leaned across the center console and pressed a kiss to my cheek. "You're the best."

MY EXPERIENCE at the pet store was a rude awakening. I had only intended to buy a bag of cat food, cat litter, and a litter box. But somehow, other items found their way into my cart. A pink collar studded with rhinestones. A plush white cat bed. Treats. Shampoo. Nail clippers. A brush and comb. A purple sweater. A pink T-shirt. A rainbow of hair bows. A purple cat carrier that looked like a designer handbag, and cost just as much as one.

A pink leash and harness.

"Really, Fancy? Is that necessary?"

"Wouldn't it be cute if I could take her for a walk around the neighborhood?"

Cute? No. It would be fucking ridiculous. It was a cat, not a goddamn dog. But then he looked at me with those eyes, and what the fuck did I know? Suddenly, a leash and harness sounded like a great idea.

Add to that at least twenty different plush and squeaky cat toys, catnip, a laser pointer, a wind-up mouse, and I shit you not, a yellow raincoat with four tiny galoshes.

"Kelley," I complained with narrowed eyes.

"What? Cats don't like water."

"Then don't fucking walk her in the rain," I reasoned.

I handed the cashier my credit card. "Your total comes to five hundred seventeen dollars and sixty-seven cents," the clerk said.

I glared evilly at Kelley. "Just the basics, huh?"

He had the decency to look contrite. "Glitter deserves the best."

So do you.

I shook my head and pocketed my wallet, feeling like a total sucker.

I loaded the bags in the bed of the truck, and as we pulled away from the store, Kelley exclaimed, "I forgot the cat tree!"

Fuck me.

"I've only been your daddy for twenty minutes and I'm already failing you," he cried to the cat. Glitter licked his nose and purred.

"You can order one online and have it delivered by tomorrow," I conceded.

Kelley booped him on the nose right back. "Your papa is the best cat dad in the world."

"Papa?"

"Yes, we need cat dad names. I'm daddy and you're papa."

Jesus H. How low would I allow myself to sink in the name of love? Lust! Or whatever the fuck I was feeling or beginning to feel.

We arrived at the dance studio, and Kelley got busy with his warm-up routine while I babysat Glitter. I felt like the world's biggest fool standing there holding a purple cat carrier that looked like a designer purse. Each one of his students that came through the door stopped to play with the cat, completely ignoring me. Which was fine with me.

Through all the countless hours I spent over the past few weeks watching how hard Kelley trained to be the best at what he did on stage, I had developed an appreciation for the skills required to perform burlesque.

"Your daddy is something else, isn't he?" I asked the cat, as if she were going to answer me. God, I was getting as bad as Kelley was.

Our second stop at the gym was no less impressive. Kelley worked hard, adding more weight to each repetition, and more repetition to each set. I hooked the cat carrier over my shoulder and held the camera in my right hand as I filmed his workout so he could upload it later. It was difficult not to remember the video of him at the gym I jerked off to without getting hard again. This was definitely not the time or the place for that.

AS SOON AS I stepped through the front doors of Limericks Sports Bar and Grille, it felt like coming home. Because it had been my second home for fifteen years. There were years, in the beginning, when I spent more time here than at my house. The decor was the same as it had been the day I first opened the doors, but everything had been replaced five years ago. New green vinyl on the barstools, a brand-new granite bar top, and a fresh coat of polyurethane on the scarred oak floors. The jukebox hadn't changed, though, and neither, it seemed, had the regular patrons.

"Graham! Where you been hiding?"

I took a deep breath and faced Limericks' most notorious customer, Murphy Maguire. "Wherever you aren't." Then I addressed his sidekick. "Hey, Hudson. You keeping him in line?"

"It's a full-time job, man. I'm doing the best I can."

"I thought if I opened a fancier location, you two would get gone, but you're still here. Where did I go wrong?"

Murphy chuffed, "That place is too fancy for us. We like it here better."

"How did I get so lucky?" I asked with a smirk.

"Murphy believes in quantity over quality," Hudson teased.

That made me laugh. "At least my liquor license isn't in jeopardy any longer since you turned twenty-one."

"Thank God for small miracles," Hudson added.

I ducked behind the bar and grabbed a bottle of water and poured it onto a small dish for Glitter. "Let her out of the bag, Kelley, so she can have a drink."

"Are you sure?"

"She can't hurt nothing. Trust me, those two don't mind," I said with a nod towards the dynamic duo sitting at the end of the bar. "They've done much worse."

Kelley unzipped the purple carrier and gently lifted the kitten out.

"Oh my gosh! Let me see!" Murphy was up and off his stool in seconds, eagerly grabbing for the cat.

"What's her name?"

"Glitter."

Murphy rubbed his cheek against the kitten's soft fur.

"She's a precious baby. I want one. River! Can—"

"No!" Hudson snapped. "Hell, you can barely take care of yourself, let alone a cat."

I couldn't hide my snicker. Hudson was absolutely correct. "Guys, this is Kelley Michaelson."

Murphy eyed Kelley appreciatively. "Oh, I know exactly who he is. I follow him on social media. We caught your show last New Year's Eve."

"Really?" Kelley lit up like a sparkler on the Fourth of July. "Thank you for following me."

Hudson laughed. "Murphy thinks he has what it takes to be a burlesque dancer."

"You weren't laughing when I wore that little red number," Murphy rebutted.

Kelley and I exchanged a secret smile and then he wisely changed the subject. "Would you like me to show you some moves?"

"Hell yeah!"

Murphy set the cat on the bar top to drink its water and tugged Kelley onto the empty dance floor.

We watched the boys dance with smiles on our faces. "You any closer to marrying him yet?"

Hudson scoffed. "Eventually. I keep waiting to see if someone beats me to it."

"You're so full of shit. He has his hooks deep into you. And you fucking love it."

Hudson chuckled and took a sip of his old-fashioned. "Yeah, I do. He's one of a kind."

I felt the exact same way about Kelley as I watched him show Murphy how to shake his ass like a pro. Did that mean I was as screwed as Hudson was?

14

KELLEY

BEING SURROUNDED by Graham's entire family was a little daunting but also, filled me with happiness. I wished I came from the kind of family that gathered to laugh and celebrate together. For now, it was enough to just be amongst them and counted as family. Even if I was only an honorary member.

Yesterday, while Graham cut the grass and cleaned the pool again, I strung tiny white lights around the umbrella that hung over the table and also around the overhang that covered the patio. I filled the common spaces in the house with freshly cut flowers from his garden and mopped the floors. As a hopeless romantic who was in love with the idea of being in love, I was beyond excited for Carson and Ryan. Celebrating their engagement gave me hope that perhaps I could be lucky enough to find love as well.

Would I be so lucky as to find it with another Carrick, like Ryan had?

All twenty of my painted fingers and toes were crossed.

Graham was dumping bags of ice into a cooler when I stepped out onto the patio dressed for the barbecue, wearing a teal bikini with loose white linen lounge pants and a long sheer white chiffon robe. My oversized straw hat and large sunglasses completed the diva look. Graham accidentally let the lid of the cooler snap closed on his hand as he ogled me.

"Ouch!" He shook his hand vigorously, never taking his eyes off me. "Damn, Fancy." He slid his hand along my hip, his thumb grazing over my bare skin in lazy strokes as he nestled in close to my neck, breathing in the scented body spray I doused myself in after my shower. "You smell delicious. Like mangoes."

His warm breath ghosted over my skin, making goosebumps pebble in his wake. I could take this man to bed right now for the rest of the day and make him late for his party.

"Do you need a hand?"

"Depends what you're offering to do with it."

I chuckled just before he stole a kiss from my lips that made my body sing. Just the touch of his lips, so soft and wet, made my body wake up and pay attention. The brush and tingle of his beard, rasping across my smooth skin, made me come alive.

"Later, when this party wraps up, I want you in my bed again. I'm going to take my time with you, love you the right way. Deep and thorough, all night long."

I gasped as he nipped my bottom lip before sucking it

into his mouth to soothe it. Damn, he had to be the sexiest man alive.

RORY AND CARLISLE were the first to arrive, and Rory and Graham got busy lighting the grill in the impressive outdoor kitchen that Graham had built with his own hands. The L-shaped polished concrete counters wrapped around a corner of the patio. I busied myself setting up a drink station on the counter while Carlisle prepped the vegetables and meats to be grilled.

Rory's injury had healed enough for him to have his stitches taken out, and he had returned to work at the lounge the previous week. It filled my heart with joy and relief to see him doing so well. He positively glowed whenever he looked at Carlisle.

The next to arrive were Graham's sisters, Gina and Gayle. Graham introduced me as his friend and houseguest, but the way his arm circled my waist possessively spoke volumes. It made all the doubts I entertained about his feelings for me solidify into a sturdy post that propped my hopeful heart up like a crutch.

Shannon and Gordy arrived about the same time, and they brought their ever-present feud with them. I sat in the shade under the umbrella and sipped my mint-infused iced tea as I watched Shannon splash in the pool. And Gordy, who sat in the shade on the lounger, pretended to be lost in his own world, but I noticed how his eyes never left Shannon. Except when Shannon looked his way. I was dying to find out what their deal was, but it wasn't really my place to ask.

Last to arrive at the party were Carson and Ryan, and judging from the dark purple bruise on Ryan's neck that looked fresh, I would hazard a guess they were late because they were necking in the car. They were so adorable. Complete opposites, but perfectly designed for each other.

It gave me hope.

Another thing that gave me hope were Graham's constant covert looks, sneaky little winks and smiles that made my stomach flip. I almost wanted to set a timer to count down to the end of the party, when we could be alone together.

I carried my drink to the pool and sat along the brick edge, pulling the hem of my pants up to my thighs and dipping my toes into the cool water. Shannon swam up to me, resting his arms on the edge of the pool to my right.

"You coming in?"

"No, just dipping my toes to cool off."

"So, tell me how you're settling in here. I haven't had a chance to ask you how you're doing."

I hadn't had the opportunity to speak with Shannon much. He was busy working the bar while I was on stage dancing. Even after my performance, when I would sit and have a drink, he was occupied with customers. Maybe I thought we wouldn't have anything in common to talk about. But I was sure that wasn't true. Besides, we had one major thing in common, we both cared very much for Graham. Shannon was an untapped well of information, a precious resource.

"I'm doing well. It's sweet of you to ask."

"I can't believe that guy got to you again in my bar.

You have no idea how mad that makes me. I'd do anything to keep you safe, I hope you know that."

My, my, these Carrick men were going to make me swoon. Though it was probably no less than he would do for anyone.

"Graham was there. He handled it. Hopefully they'll catch him soon."

"I hope so, too." He hesitated, continuing to stare at me, and I knew he had more to say. "What are you going to do then? You gave up your apartment. Will you find a new place?"

I tucked my hair behind my ear and kicked my feet, making small waves in the water. "Eventually."

Shannon looked over my shoulder, and I knew he was glancing at his father. "I don't think he wants you to be in any kind of rush. Maybe take your time and make sure you're doing the right thing."

What point was he trying to make? "And what is the right thing?"

"I guess whatever keeps you safe and makes you happy."

"What if I'm happy right here?"

"Then you should stay. Maybe that's what's best for everyone."

I looked up into the sun and closed my eyes, enjoying the warmth on my face. He was giving me permission to stay, to do as I pleased. To do what felt right. I hadn't realized until now that I wanted and needed his acceptance. But I did. And I think Graham needed it more. I only hoped Shannon gave it to him as well.

I turned my attention back to Shannon. "Thank you. You have no idea how much I needed to hear that."

I was about to ask for insider information when the man in question squatted down next to me. Graham held a plate in his hands loaded with raw vegetables, cut fresh fruit, and a hot dog that looked a little too white to be authentic.

"Made you a Tofurkey dog, hot off the grill. Not that it makes it taste any better," he teased.

I accepted the plate with a smile. "You are sweet as sugar. What are you going to eat?"

"I scarfed down a Tofurkey dog while I was manning the grill. I'm trying to save room for my sister's chocolate cake."

"Pops, you ate Tofurkey? I never thought I'd see the day."

Graham smirked in spite of the red tint creeping over his neck. "Yeah well, Kelley keeps harassing me about my cholesterol and blood pressure. Something about heart disease, yada yada yada. It's easier to just eat it than listen to him go on and on."

He didn't stick around to hear Shannon's opinion. But that didn't stop Shannon from sharing it with me.

An amused smile touched his lips. "You're good for him, you know that? There's not one person in this backyard that could have gotten him to eat that damn fake meat except you."

He hoisted himself over the edge of the pool, water sluicing down his fit body, and grabbed a towel. I smiled to myself, thinking about his words. Maybe I was good for Graham. Maybe I was just what he needed.

15

GRAHAM

I'D BEEN WAITING for this day. Counting down to it since my best friend had his stitches taken out. Rory called me yesterday and said he was finally ready to take his bike out on the road again. So I called Shannon, since we were both off today, and we made plans to ride down to the beach and grab lunch on the boardwalk. We'd done it a hundred times, but this wasn't like any of those. Today was brand new. Carlisle and Kelley were joining us for the first time.

The weather was perfect, a slight breeze kept the sun's direct rays from scorching us. I tossed water bottles to Shannon and Rory and tucked two into my saddlebags. Kelley stepped through the garage door looking like he was dressed to go anywhere but riding. I heard Shannon and Rory snicker as I took it all in. Kelley was dressed in painted-on white jeans that he tucked into black boots, but not the kind meant for riding motorcycles. Certainly not. These were studded with rhinestones and might have been made of suede. He wore a white tank top that someone had bedazzled the shit out of, and a purple leather jacket.

But that wasn't the part that had me shaking my head. He was holding Glitter cuddled against his chest.

"Are we ready?" he asked, perfectly serious.

"The cat cannot come with us. You're gonna have to leave her here."

He looked crushed. "I'm sorry, baby girl. Papa says you can't come. No kitties on the bikes. I won't be gone long, I promise." He dashed back through the door, and I could just feel the unspoken opinions gathering momentum behind my back, like a snowball rolling down a hill.

"Thought you said you'd never get a cat because cats were for pansies."

"Fuck off, Shannon," I said without heat.

He only laughed. "It's good to see you happy," he said, clapping me on the back.

"I've always been happy."

"Yeah, but now you're in love."

I frowned hard. "I didn't say anything about love."

"You didn't have to. It's written all over your face."

I blew out a gusty breath, my shoulders sagging. "Fuck me. I feel ridiculous. It doesn't bother you that he's so much younger? Younger than you even."

"Fuck no. Who cares? There are only two things that are important to me. Number one, does he make you happy? And I can clearly see he does."

"What's the second thing?"

"That he's a good guy and he's not taking advantage of you. But Kelley isn't like that."

That gave me a modicum of hope. Kelley re-emerged, and I grabbed the extra helmet sitting on the pillion seat of my bike and handed it to him. He balked at it like it was covered in ants.

"I have to wear that?"

"Of course. Your safety is more important than your looks, Fancy. No helmet, no bike."

"Ugh! It's my hair I'm worried about, not my looks." With his hands on his hips, he shook his head sadly. "I'll be right back."

When he returned five minutes later, he drew a whistle from Rory. Kelley had added a purple zebra print silk scarf over his hair that he'd tied under his chin. Coupled with large purple sunglasses, he looked like Marilyn frickin' Monroe or some shit.

"Damn, Pops, you really got the pick of the litter. Kudos," he congratulated me in a low voice, looking slightly amused but also impressed.

Was my kid really impressed with me? Damn, if he wasn't stroking my ego today.

I placed the helmet on Kelley's head and buckled it under his chin. He swallowed and stared directly into my eyes.

"Is it too much?" His voice was a soft whisper.

He was really asking if *he* was too much.

I stared right back, my words ghosting over his glossy lips like a caress. "You could never be too much, Fancy. You're nothing but perfect."

. . .

THE WIND FELT cool on my face as we cruised down the strip that separated the ocean from the boardwalk lined with restaurants and shops. The weight of Kelley's body warmed my back, his hands clasped tightly over my stomach. Every time I caught a glimpse of his face in my side view mirrors, he was smiling. He looked so beautiful, euphoric even, with the sun and the wind kissing his face. For as fancy as I teased him of being, Kelley was a very down-to-earth guy who loved the simple things in life. The things that held the most value, like enjoying a beautiful day with friends, being surrounded by family, laughter and love. All the core values I held dear.

We turned off into a small public parking lot and parked the bikes. I helped Kelley remove his helmet, sneaking a covert glance at the boys to make sure their eyes were not on us before popping a quick kiss to his lips. His brilliant smile displaced everything in my chest, turning it upside down and sideways.

"Hey, Pops," Shannon called as he hung his helmet on the handlebars of his bike. "Do you want to hit up that little shack that sells wraps?"

"That sounds great," Rory seconded.

"Sure," I agreed, fully aware that my first thought was whether they had something Kelley would enjoy. It was so natural to me now to put his needs and wants before my own. As natural as breathing.

Shannon walked ahead of us with Carly and Rory behind him holding hands. Kelley and I trailed behind, close enough that our shoulders and arms brushed against each other, and my fingers itched to take his hand in mine. I was sure he didn't have a problem with public displays of affection because he was naturally a touchy-feely kind of guy, but I wasn't so sure how he felt about displaying that affection toward me specifically. The sex we'd been having was on a different level than hand holding and kissing in public. That was something we did in the bedroom, behind closed doors.

If I were being honest, I was thinking of how others would react to our age difference. Compounded by the fact that we were both men. It was something I hadn't had to think about since...ever, really. I thought maybe those things didn't matter so much to Kelley. He was so brave performing in front of others, venturing out into public dressed the way he was. It was hard to believe someone who wore such gender fluid clothing cared about the opinions of others. But it was also a human failing to feel the sting of rejection, and I didn't want to exacerbate that for him.

And if I wanted to dig a little deeper, I could admit that it made me feel a little ridiculous, pathetic even, to flaunt such a young man on my arm, such a pretty man. Did it make me look like a perverted old fool? I thought maybe it did, but that was probably just my own insecurity.

It was definitely an issue I was going to have to reconcile if I wanted to pursue something more permanent with Kelley, which I definitely did.

He brushed his fingers against mine every few steps, stealing shy glances in my direction and secret smiles that made my heart beat faster. Never in my fifty-three years had I been the recipient of such flirtatious affection, and it felt fucking amazing. Having Kelley's undivided attention focused on me was like drinking from the fountain of youth. I felt younger, lighter—invincible.

Like a fucking teenager with his first crush.

The Wrap Shack was a little vendor cart parked along the boardwalk that sold a variety of mouthwatering wraps and sandwiches. I usually went for the El Pastor, seasoned and braised pork with shredded cabbage slaw marinated in a chipotle cream sauce. But with Kelley's voice in my head, urging me to be mindful of my health, I chose the California club instead, same as Kelley did. Shannon snickered, but screw him. The roasted veggies and creamy garlic sauce tasted delicious. I barely even missed the meat.

"I think I'll have one of those as well," Rory added. I hid my smile by biting into my wrap. The poor schmuck was in the same boat as me, trying to keep up with a younger man and maintain his physique and his health. This whole dating-a-younger-man thing was no joke. I was going to have to change a lot of my stubborn bachelor ways if I wanted to maintain my Zaddy status.

It seemed like Rory was going to be my accountability partner, so at least I wouldn't be suffering alone.

We ate as we walked, and about half a mile down the boardwalk, Rory lifted his arm to chuck his wrapper into the nearest trash can, like he was shooting a basketball into a net, and winced, his face screwing up tight.

"Are you okay?" I lifted the hem of his T-shirt to look at his scar, but it looked healed over. Dark reddish-purple and angry, but not bleeding.

"Yeah," he assured me, tugging his shirt back down. "I'm fine, but the riding gets to me."

"If it gets to be too much, we can head back. Just say the word."

"Nah, I'm fine. I wouldn't trade this beautiful day for anything. I'm gonna take a walk over there with Carly," he said, pointing to a clearing on the beach not heavily populated by tourists and families.

Shannon was on a phone call. I placed my hand over the small of Kelley's back. "Take a walk with me."

We found an empty picnic table, and I sat on the tabletop with my feet on the bench, looking out over the water. The sun was lower on the horizon, almost touching the water's edge. It was a beautiful sight. Kelley sat on the bench, to the left of my feet, and I tugged him over to sit between my legs, caging him in with my knees. I leaned forward, bringing my mouth even with his ear, and pressed a kiss to the soft spot behind his lobe. He smelled like watermelon today, and I breathed him in deep, letting his scent wash over my nerves like a balm.

"It's beautiful, isn't it?"

He was referring to the view, but I only had eyes for him. "Mmm, very beautiful."

When I nipped at his earlobe, he giggled and tipped his head back to stare up into my eyes. "I like riding with you. Sitting behind you on the bike as it rumbles beneath us, clinging onto you like my big strong teddy bear. I could get used to that."

His words made my heart sing. As different as we were, it was a relief to discover we had so many things in common. I removed his sunglasses and pressed a kiss to his forehead. Kelley sat up and swung his legs so his body was facing me with his legs under the table. He wrapped his arms around my waist and tilted his face up to mine. It was all the invitation I needed.

I lowered my head and brushed my lips across his, waiting for him to open for me. He parted them on a breathy sigh, full of pleasure, and I slid my tongue inside his mouth. Kelley licked at my tongue, sucking on it with teasing pulls, and it was hard not to imagine how it would feel on my cock. My stomach swirled as I tasted him, and thoughts of wanting more danced in my head. My fingers gripped the back of his neck, pulling him into me. His warm wet mouth embraced my tongue eagerly, and my entire world was reduced to the exquisiteness of his soft mouth. All too soon, I pulled my tongue back, and we shared sweet nips and sucks with our kiss-swollen lips.

"I don't want this to end," he breathed in a soft whisper.

Me either. "Eventually, the sun is going to set, and I don't like riding in the dark."

"No, I mean this," he gestured between us. "You and me. I don't want this to end between us. You probably think I'm too young with a silly crush, but I'm not. I don't want casual. I don't want temporary."

I swallowed, feeling a heavy weight settle on my chest. "What do you want?" I rasped.

"You. Us. A future. I don't want to play games with you. I want to lay all my cards out on the table and be straightforward."

Fuck me, were we really discussing this? My heart beat painfully hard. "Okay, lay them out. Let me see your hand."

"This thing between us we've been building, I think

it's enough to make things work. I know you have reservations about the difference between our ages and our lifestyles." He pursed his glossy lips and shook his head. "Can you honestly tell me you don't want this?"

I couldn't say any such thing. "Kelley—"

"No. The truth, Graham."

Here we go. Time to gamble with my heart. Again.

"I want this. I want you."

He smiled. "Was that so hard?"

"Terrifying." I smirked.

When I had him in my arms like this, with my lips pressed against his warm skin, it was easy to see a future for us. To believe in forever and happy endings. But when I let him go, the space created between our bodies was just enough to let all the doubts and insecurities seep in.

It came down to a matter of faith. Kelley had faith in me. He believed in us. And I believed in him. Everything else was a risk, but that's what life was, a series of risks. And in my experience, a life without risks wasn't worth living.

"You sure about this? You really think you want me? I have a loud family, two bars to run, gray hair, and a bad back."

"Sounds like heaven. You're aging like a fine wine. And you taste just as delicious," he teased, brushing his lips across mine. His breath tasted sweet and warm, and I couldn't stop myself from stealing another kiss.

"Will you move your things into my bedroom?"

"As soon as we get home." He grinned against my lips. It was infectious, causing me to grin even wider.

"Then let's hurry up and get the fuck home."

He moved to stand, but I tugged him back down between my legs and buried my face in his neck, inhaling his sweet fragrance one more time. He giggled and pulled me closer.

"I'm falling so hard for you, Fancy. Hard and fast. Don't let me hit the ground."

"Hopefully, you'll land right on top of me, where you belong."

16

KELLEY

I WAS up with the sun after having slept like a baby. The reassurances we agreed upon yesterday, regarding the status of our relationship, was the best melatonin. I showered, shaved, and spritzed myself with summer peaches body spray because it drove me absolutely wild when Graham nuzzled my neck and groaned like he wanted to eat me alive.

I felt brighter than sunshine in my sunny yellow lace blouse tucked into white high-waisted short shorts. My legs were shaved smooth and rubbed with lotion until they shone, and on my feet, I wore white canvas wedges that tied like ballet flats around my ankles.

It was difficult to prepare breakfast without making noise, but I wanted Graham to sleep in as late as he could. It was the smell of sizzling turkey bacon and freshly ground coffee that finally woke him. He shuffled into the kitchen, his hair a spiky mess, wearing nothing but black boxer briefs. His inked skin was on full display, but my eyes were drawn to the black cotton-covered bulge between his thick thighs.

I would *never* not be attracted to this man.

And the first thing he did, to my everlasting delight, was fold me into his arms and bury his face in my neck, inhaling me like breakfast.

"You look delicious, sunshine. And so pretty," he noted, pulling away to look down at my outfit. "But don't you have class today?"

"I did, but my dance class was canceled. One student is studying for exams, two are out of town, and one is sick. That only leaves me with two students, which isn't enough to cover the classroom rental fee for the day."

"I'll gladly cover the fee if you want to practice," he suggested, nipping at my earlobe.

He unleashed a swarm of butterflies in my stomach when he said things like that, especially when he said them while kissing on me. I've had men buy me a drink or buy me something pretty to wear that they wanted to see me in, but everything they'd given me was for their benefit, not mine. Graham offered me things that benefited him in no way whatsoever. His generosity was solely for my happiness. It was the kind of selfless love I had dreamed of receiving my entire life. All the romcoms and Disney movies I drooled over, while thinking they were nothing but silly fantasies, were finally coming true with Graham. It was just more proof that I had found the right man.

"I appreciate that, but I think I'll decline. Sometimes, it's nice to have a day off. A day where I can spend more time with you."

"Don't you have to perform tonight?"

"I do. Until then, I just want you to relax and let me pamper you."

"How is that relaxing for you?" He laughed and stroked his fingers across my cheek.

"I have too much energy to sit around and do nothing. I can't think of anything that would make me happier or give me more pleasure than waiting on you hand and foot today." He looked skeptical. "Not because I feel like I have to. But because I'm *dying* to." I fixed him a cup of coffee just how he liked it, as black as his motorcycle, and shooed him from the kitchen. "Go and sit. I grabbed your newspaper from outside. It's on the coffee table waiting for you. Breakfast is almost ready."

He stopped in the doorway and turned back, gazing at me softly. "I know I don't deserve you. But I thank God every day that I found you." And then he disappeared, leaving me to melt in a puddle of goo from his words.

I had it so fucking bad for him.

After breakfast, I treated Graham to some morning stretching where he pretended to read the newspaper while covertly watching my ass as I bent over. I had finally gotten him to admit it was his favorite part of the day. While he showered and dressed, I strapped the pink harness and leash on Glitter and took her for a walk. The leash was completely unnecessary. She followed me everywhere, nipping at my heels like a puppy. She was the best kitten baby a guy could ask for. Glitter stopped to look up at every tree we passed, probably searching out birds.

I waved to Mrs. Warren, Graham's neighbor two

houses down. I hadn't admitted this to him, but his neighborhood was the perfect quintessential backdrop for all of my daydreams whenever I pictured my ideal perfect life. I could see myself here, be ridiculously happy here, with Graham and Glitter. Sunset walks, sharing the yard work on the weekends, washing my car while he tinkered with his bike. It all came together effortlessly in my mind.

When we returned home, I wiped her paws clean, served her breakfast, and then cleaned up the kitchen. As I was loading the dishwasher, Graham snuck up behind me and wrapped his arms around my waist. I sighed with pleasure from those big strong arms that held me tight. He planted soft wet kisses on my neck that made shivers of delight skate down my spine. He was being extra affectionate today, and I guessed it was because he was allowing himself to feel his feelings now that he wasn't so worried about where we stood. I was grateful for the change in him. For a cuddle bug like me, there was no such thing as too many hugs and kisses.

We ended up on the patio, enjoying the morning shade on the padded loungers. I reached over and grabbed Graham's feet and placed them in my lap, treating him to a foot massage. He purred like a kitten, louder than Glitter when I rubbed her belly. He tipped his head back and closed his eyes, smiling contentedly.

"What color would you like to see me wear tonight when I dance for you?"

He lifted his head and blinked his eyes open. A wicked heat burned their depths. "Red. You look hot as fuck in red. With that lipstick and the nail polish to match, you make my cock so fucking hard."

Red, it is, I smiled to myself. I had a surprise for him tonight that was so hot it was going to scorch his short and curlies.

I HAD no intention of letting him see my outfit before I took the stage, so I hid behind a white sweatsuit. The rest of my accessories, including my heels, were stowed in my duffel bag. I'd chosen a ruby-red satin corset with matching panties. A black satin garter belt cinched my waist and hooked onto black fishnet stockings. On my feet, I wore black patent leather stilettos, and I tied a red satin scarf around my neck like a bow. It was the highlight of my outfit and my performance tonight. I had plans for that red satin sash that would hopefully cause Graham to nearly come in his pants right there in front of everyone.

I waved to Shannon and Carson behind the bar as I passed it on my way to the hallway behind the stage where I kept my duffel while I performed. Graham escorted me. I shook my head at him.

"No peeking tonight. I want to surprise you. Go wait for me on the other side of the stage, please."

He looked around, checking both ends of the corridor. "Listen, I need you to be on guard. Extra vigilant. It's been a while since his last attempt on you, and—" He shivered like a bad feeling crawled up his spine, "—I don't know, just a feeling in my gut, but I think he's going to make another move soon."

"Really?" Unease swirled in my gut.

"I wouldn't put it past him. He wants you, and he's not going to give up easily. Promise me, extra vigilant."

"I promise."

Graham popped a kiss to my lips and disappeared through the side door next to the stage. I would see him on the other side, after I transformed into a siren. A rush of anticipation and excitement moved through me as I slipped out of my sweats. Unzipping my duffel bag, I carefully folded my clothes and laid them on top, then grabbed my heels and exchanged them with my sneakers, shoving them into the bag with less finesse. A deep breath in through my nose, held in my chest until the count of ten, and then released through my mouth in a slow exhale, calmed the spike of adrenaline stimulating my heart. I waited until the music cued me and slipped through the black velvet curtain, taking my place under the muted glow of the stage lights.

A single black wooden chair waited for me center stage. I stood behind it and gripped the top, and when the initial applause died down, I hooked my leg around the chair and planted my heel on the woven cane seat. I ran my hands down my thigh, teasing the edge of the stocking with my bright red fingernails.

And when I looked up into the audience, Graham's eyes stared back at me. I had his full attention.

I trailed my hand down to my ankle and slowly dragged it back up again before lowering my leg to the stage and twirling around the chair in circles. Dancing on the balls of my feet, I used the chair as I would a pole, if this were that kind of dance, and moved fluidly. I gripped the seat of the chair, squatted down to the ground, and popped back up again with my legs slightly spread, showing the crowd an enticing view of my ass.

Taking a seat on it, I worked through a routine of sexy chair dancing moves I'd practiced for hours the previous week. Lifting each of my legs in turn, sliding my fingers down the long length of them, dragging them down my black satin elbow-length gloves, the same ones Graham had used to bring himself off with. I caught his gaze, silently reminding him of the memory. The heat in his eyes told me he remembered crystal clear.

Damn, what I wouldn't give to see him do that.

I spun my body and straddled the back of the chair, rising up slightly, the muscles in my thighs flexing as I rode the chair, up and down as if I were fucking it. Leaning back to show off the taught line of my torso, I closed my eyes and smiled as the ends of the red satin bow around my neck tickled my face.

The appeal of burlesque was all about highlighting the human body. The legs, feet, arms, neck, hands. The stomach and back, hips and rear. The secret was to showcase them in a way that elevated them from simple anatomy to erotic and irresistible.

Easier said than done.

I sat up slowly and lifted my leg in a seated leg kick, bringing my knee even with my mouth. Again, I caught Graham's gaze, suddenly wishing we were the only two people in the room. I'd give anything to fuck him in this chair, to ride him under the stage lights, in sync with the driving beat of the music. And that's when a thought occurred to me. I decided to improvise my routine, which I never did. I was carried away by my fantasy, inspired by the hunger in Graham's shamrock green eyes. I pointed at him and curled my finger, inviting him closer. His eyes bugged out, and I hid my laugh behind a sly curve of my red lips and nodded.

"Come here," I mouthed silently.

He looked around him before hopping up on the stage effortlessly, which looked so fucking sexy. "You okay?" he whispered in my ear.

I stood and gripped his shirt, gently pushing him down into the chair. "Sit."

Graham sat and stared up at me hesitantly. He had to be wondering what I had in store for him. Why keep him guessing? I lifted my leg, bending it at the knee, and rested my black heel on his thigh. His eyes strayed to the place between my thighs covered in red satin. If I'd known beforehand I was going to tease myself during my performance, I would have taped my dick down. It was thickening now, and I hoped it wouldn't embarrass me. Much. I let go of his shirt and trailed my fingers down his chest, down his stomach that flexed under my touch, over my foot, and up my leg. He tracked the path of my fingernails, his lips slightly parted. I imagined his heart was beating much faster now, anticipating my next move.

Slowly, I untied the sash around my neck and slithered it over his lap, up his chest. Originally, I had planned to do a bit of a ribbon dance with it, but this was much hotter. I stood straight, removing my foot from his thigh, and twirled around him as the satin draped over him. I ended up behind his chair and pulled the sash slowly up his chest, tickling his neck with the ends. He gasped when I grasped his wrists and drew them behind the chair. I tied them together with the ribbon, making him my prisoner for the remainder of my performance.

With my fingers carding through his hair, I gripped the ends slightly and tugged, tipping his head back to see his face. The heat in his eyes intensified, and he licked his lips. I smiled and dipped my head closer to his before pulling away like a tease.

Moving around to the front of the chair, I performed a series of sensual squats before crawling between his parted legs. With my hands planted on his knees, I crawled up Graham's body and walked my fingers down his chest again. His erection was blatant, pushing against the thick denim of his jeans. I wanted nothing more than to rub on it until I got both of us off. But that would have to wait until later, when we were alone. I slid off his body, needing to put some distance between us while we both cooled off, and did a floor routine of splits, swirls, and leg lifts while seated on my butt.

When I returned to Graham, I untied his wrists and teased the tip of the sash over his lips. "Bite," I commanded.

With wide eyes, he took the red satin between his teeth. I took the other end between mine and with my fingers, slowly tugged him to me, closer and closer to my mouth, until only an inch separated us. I took the sash from his mouth and dropped my end as well, and brushed my lips over his in a soft kiss. It was only a featherlight caress, but it made every cell in my body vibrate with need.

"Take me home," I whispered against his lips.

I stood and took a bow before waving at the crowd.

The applause was deafening, especially from the squealing ladies. I smiled and soaked it up. This was the second-best part of performing; the first being the physical satisfaction of pushing my body and the burn in my muscles. I slipped behind the curtain, Graham right behind me, and checked the hallway cautiously before going to my duffel bag. He slammed into me from behind, and I hit the wall with a thud, laughing breathlessly. Graham caged me in by putting his hands on the wall on either side of my head. He dipped his mouth to mine, breathing over my lips, his eyes trained on them. I swiped my tongue over them to drive him mad.

"Such a fucking tease," he growled.

"Me?"

"Don't play coy, Fancy. You got me all worked up and then begged me to take you home. And guess what we're gonna do now."

"Um, go home?"

"Not yet, baby." His voice was a menacing whisper that made my cock all the way hard. "I've got to help out around here first while you park your pretty ass on a barstool." He brushed his lips over mine, pulling away before I could chase him, and leaned back, looking into my eyes with a wicked smirk. "I'm gonna hold on to this for a little while. Behave yourself."

He tucked the red sash into his back pocket with a wink. Great! He'd turned the tables on me, and now I was the one being teased out of my mind with sexual anticipation. How in the hell had that happened?

17

GRAHAM

IT WASN'T ABSOLUTELY necessary for me to hang around the lounge after his performance, but I figured it couldn't hurt. Kelley had dragged me up onto the stage in front of everyone and teased the fuck out of my cock until I was rock hard and aching for him, and now he was going to know what it felt like to sit in a room surrounded by strangers with a hard cock, full of need.

Sometimes, payback could be a real bitch. So could sitting around making small talk while you were desperate to come.

While I made myself busy in the back, sorting and stacking boxes of supplies and restocking the bar area, Kelley found an empty stool next to Ryan. I spied a couple of empty shot glasses lined up in front of them.

From experience, I knew Ryan was a lush when he drank. Not that I wanted to think about that too much. But I did wonder what kind of drunk Kelley was. I'd never seen him tipsy before, and I was more than a little curious to find out what would happen to his personality when it was soaked in alcohol. Just a smidge, not too much. As I stocked napkins and drink stirrers underneath the counter, I watched as he knocked back two more shots, thinking I would get the chance to find out tonight.

Over the next hour, I paid careful attention as his laugh became a bit louder, his smile a little wider, and the looks he gave me lingered a lot longer.

Yep, another lush.

That would suit me just fine because I had plans for him when we got home. Plans that involved red satin.

But it seemed he couldn't wait until we got home. Kelley began his sensual assault in the truck by trailing his fingers up my thigh as I drove.

"Careful," I chuckled. "You're playing with fire."

"Mmm, good thing you have a big extinguisher handy." He rubbed his palm over my erection and squeezed.

Such a fucking tease, but I was going to have the last word tonight. He just didn't know it yet. My head was filled with dozens of filthy ideas, things I'd wanted to do to him for weeks now, and tonight, I would give myself license to explore every one of them.

I spread my thighs wider, inviting him to touch me. "That was some performance you did tonight. Had you practiced that?"

"Not really. I was only going to dance with the ribbon. Do some sexy chair moves, but solo."

"What made you add me?"

His eyes twinkled as they stared into mine. "You inspired me. The way you watched me. It drove me crazy."

"Did it?"

"I wanted to fuck you in that chair."

"Damn, Kelley. That would be...something else." Christ, the visual had me rock hard.

I covered his hand with mine, urging him to press harder. He leaned across the seat and sucked on my ear, tracing the shell with his warm tongue. "Is that what you're going to do to me when we get home?"

He breathed the words in my ear, a whispered suggestion of sin and pleasure, and my hand came up to cup his cheek and press his mouth to my neck. Kelley sucked on the unshaven skin, no doubt leaving marks behind to show his claim on me. It was clear as day if you just looked close enough. It was in the constant soft smile I sported, the laughter that came easily and often these days, and in the sappy expression I wore whenever I looked at him.

Yeah, Kelley Michaelson had definitely left his mark on me.

And I wore it proudly.

Just fucking look at him. Who wouldn't be proud to have him? With the gorgeous face of a model and the jacked body of an athlete, the carefully applied makeup that accentuated his beauty and the clothes that made him look hella fucking sexy, it was next to impossible not to be attracted to him.

"That and more," I growled.

AS SOON AS the front door closed behind us, I locked it, engaged the alarm, and grabbed for him, pulling him into my arms. I was starved for his kiss. My mouth sucked everywhere, his lips, his tongue, cheeks, neck, wherever my mouth landed, I tasted, feasting on his sweet smooth flesh.

"Lose the sweats and get in my bed."

"*Our* bed," he clarified, which drove me fucking nuts.

Kelley shed clothes as he went, leaving a trail behind him for me to follow.

"Leave everything black and red on," I barked.

I walked slowly, giving him a minute to get settled before joining him. He stole my breath when I walked into the bedroom. Kelley was sprawled seductively on the bed, dressed like a wet fucking dream. He still wore his heels. I stalked him like prey, coming closer to the bed as I whipped my shirt over my head. His eyes immediately dropped to my chest. What he saw in me, I didn't know, but I knew he loved whatever it was. His pupils dilated, and he licked his red lips. Like he couldn't wait to taste me. I knew exactly how he felt. When I finally got my mouth on him, I wasn't going to stop. Ever.

I unbuttoned my jeans and lowered the zipper, drawing his gaze lower, but I left them on my hips. His eyes widened when I pulled the red sash from my back pocket and planted a knee on the bed.

"What are you going to do with that?"

Perversely, I asked, "What would you like me to do with it?"

His breath caught. "I have so many ideas."

"Me, too. Lay on your back." I crawled between his spread thighs and planted my knees on either side of his hips, straddling his pelvis, and gathered his wrists together. "I don't have bars or posts on my headboard to tie you to, so I'll have to improvise." I tied the sash around his wrists and tested the knot. "That should hold you. Keep them above your head and out of my way."

He kept his eyes trained on my face as he complied, and his knees fell farther apart. "I like these," I said, tracing my fingertip down his satin-covered bulge. My touch was soft, a slow, maddening descent toward his sac. He squirmed, rolling his hips. "So pretty. So sexy. Until I'd seen them on you, I had no idea how much I liked seeing pretty things dressing up a man's cock."

"Graham—"

I had no idea what he was asking for, but I was determined to give it to him, anyway. I rubbed my fingers back and forth over the red satin, addicted to the feel of it, so smooth and silky over his hot hard dick. I could feel the heat of him through the flimsy fabric and see the wetness staining the material. He was begging for my touch.

"Please."

"Please what?"

"Touch me."

"I am." My smile was wicked.

"Harder. I need more. You're teasing me."

"Like you teased me tonight? In front of everyone?"

"I'm sorry. I can make it up to you. With my mouth."

"I know you can. And you will. After I've made you beg."

"I am begging, Graham. Please."

"Not hard enough. I don't see tears in your eyes yet."

His pretty blue eyes rounded wide. He was finally starting to imagine what I had in store for him tonight.

I rubbed over his sac, tickling with my barely-there touch, until I brushed over his taint and pressed against the smooth honey-colored skin. I couldn't see it, but I could easily recall what it looked like the last time I had my mouth on him. My fingers dropped to his crease, the satin so thin it molded between his cheeks. Kelley lifted his hips off the bed, silently begging me to play with his ass.

Silent wasn't going to work for me tonight. I wanted to hear him, loud and clear.

"I bet I could bring you off from just rubbing you like this."

"You could," he gasped, the muscles in his stomach flexing as he writhed.

I dropped my mouth to his groin and stretched my lips over the ridge of his erection. I mouthed his panties, breathing hot air over the damp fabric, tasting the spot where his precum had soiled the satin. He dropped his hands to my head, pushing my face between his parted thighs.

"Touch me and I stop. Move your arms back up to the headboard and behave yourself."

A whining moan tore from his throat as he complied. I licked a wet trail with my tongue down his rigid length, teasing him, knowing he wished there were no barrier between my mouth and his skin. With my teeth, I nipped the sensitive flesh of his inner thigh, causing him to cry out my name.

I chuckled. I was just getting started with him.

Leaving the garter belt on, I peeled the edge of his panties down his hips, barely exposing the base of his dick, and sucked hard there. Kelley's body jackknifed off the bed as his upper body raised up.

"Lie down." My voice was in no way gentle.

I tugged his panties down his hips, down his thighs, and over his heels. But instead of tossing them to the floor, I wadded them in my fist and circled his cock, using the damp satin as a cock sleeve as I stroked him. Clear salty pearls dripped from his slit, soaking into the fabric. I swiped the next one with my tongue, and he cried out.

"Give me your mouth. Suck on me," he demanded.

"I'm done having you call the shots tonight. We're doing this my way, Fancy."

I licked his balls, bathing them in my saliva, as I jacked his shaft. They felt so smooth and soft against my tongue. Squeezing with my lips, I applied the barest pressure to his sac. Kelley chanted my name over and over.

"Graham. Graham. Graham."

A soft plea, begging for mercy.

I raised up and stuffed the silken wad into his mouth, and before he could object, I bent his knees, folding his body in half, and settled between his legs once more. My tongue came out to play, dragging through his crease. I pressed the tip against his soft pink pucker. His muffled cries sounded like they were begging for more, but I couldn't be sure. I stiffened my tongue and pushed it into his hole, pressing in as deep as I could before sliding back out. Again and again, I repeated the move until the sounds he made blended into one long continuous stream. I looked up from between his legs and saw fresh tears rolling down his blushed cheeks. The insides of his creamy thighs were red and aggravated from the abrasive scruff of my beard, and I soothed the abused skin with my tongue. He squeezed his powerful thighs closed around my head, trapping my mouth against his sensitive flesh.

He was ready.

I was beyond ready.

I sat up and wiggled out of my jeans and briefs, tossing them aside, and crawled up the length of his body, settling my weight over him. Bringing my face to his, I pegged him with hard, hungry eyes.

"I'm going to slide into you. Keep your hands where they are."

It was a sacrifice to forgo the feel of him beneath me as I sat up and reached over to the top drawer in my nightstand to grab a condom. While rolling it on, I asked, "Do you need lube?" Last time I'd asked, he'd gotten huffy. This time, he pleaded with his eyes, frantically shaking his head. I took the panties from his mouth.

"No lube," he rasped. "I'm wet enough from your tongue. I want to really feel it."

"Oh, you're going to, I promise."

I stretched out over him and grasped his tied wrists in my fist, holding them hostage above his head. My other hand cupped his cheek. In between the words I spoke, I teased his lips with kisses.

"When you're ready to come, tell me. I want it down my throat."

He nodded and pushed his dick against mine, seeking friction like a kitten rubbing against a scratching post.

I kissed him deeply, rubbing my tongue over his as I pressed the fat head of my cock against his tight pucker. With a grunt, I pushed inside his incredible heat.

"Graham!"

"I'm here, baby doll. Fuck, you feel amazing." My lips landed on his cheeks, his nose, his chin, as I slid in and out of his tight passage. "So fucking beautiful," I said gazing into his glassy eyes. "I'm going to make a mess of that pretty face when I come all over it."

He gasped, his eyes widening at my words. I increased my pace, pushing into his body harder with each thrust. The stroke of my cock in his velvet channel, the way his ass squeezed my shaft so tight, choking the blood flow from it, weakened my resolve to last longer than three minutes. My hips pistoned in and out of his ass, and he bent his knees up to his shoulders, opening his whole body up to my forceful invasion.

He fucking loved it. His breathless moans of pleasure drowned out the sound of my own harsh breathing, filling my head with carnal thoughts. I couldn't get deep enough, not in his ass or his mouth or his heart. I wanted to crawl inside of him and take over every part of him.

"Fuck. I'm so close. Tell me you're close."

"I am. If you want it, come get it. Hurry."

With a curse, I pulled from his body and crawled down between his thighs. His dick was engorged, dark red, veins bulging, the tip a soaked and sticky mess. I took it between my lips, right to the back of my throat, and swallowed around his shaft repeatedly until he cried out my name and flooded my throat with his release. It burned, hot and bitter, and I swallowed every delicious drop.

Quickly, I raised up on my knees and crawled up his chest. I stroked my dick as I stared down into his eager face. He was starving for my load. It only took three pumps before I shot thick white ropes over his face, his cheeks and bright red lips marked with my seed. Kelley opened his mouth and caught the last spurt on his pink tongue. I pushed the slippery head of my cock between his lips, and he sucked, making sure to milk every drop from my shaft. Then, I pulled out and rubbed the sensitive head over his wet lips. He puckered them, and the sight drove me crazy.

My pounding pulse gradually settled into a normal rhythm and I leaned over the edge of the mattress, grabbing my discarded shirt and wiping his face clean. I laid next to him and pulled him into my arms. Kelley rolled, lying his head on my chest, and bent his knee over my thighs. His contented sigh filled my heart.

"Can you untie my wrists now?"

I laughed, having completely forgotten. As I loosened the knot, I said, "I hope you meant what you said about settling down with me. Because I can't imagine ever being able to let you go."

He rotated his wrists to loosen them up and then raised up over me and looked into my face. "I meant every word. I'm not going anywhere. Ever. You're stuck with me and Glitter, for better or worse."

Sounds fucking perfect.

18

KELLEY

SINCE ACQUIRING Graham as my constant shadow, the best part about working out, for me, was having his total attention for the entire two hours. I loved having his eyes on me while my muscles flexed and strained in the best ways. He never failed to get hard from watching me, which was the best foreplay.

We pushed through the front doors of the gym and were assaulted by the familiar scent of sweat and disinfectant. I bypassed all the workout equipment and made a beeline for the locker room.

"I'm just going to stow my duffel bag in a locker and change. Meet me in the sauna?"

"The sauna?"

I rolled my shoulders. "I'm feeling really tight. Must be from having my arms tied above my head for most of the night." I flashed him a dirty smile. "The heat from the sauna will help loosen my muscles before I start working out, so I don't pull something. Plus, it will make my body nice and sweaty and shiny, which looks great on camera when you film me."

Graham grimaced, looking left and right before discreetly adjusting his dick. "Damn, Kelley. You're just begging to get tied up again."

"I'll see you in a minute, sugar," I said, kissing him on the cheek. "Why don't you grab us some towels and meet me by the sauna?"

As I walked away, I glanced back over my shoulder once and smiled. Even in sweatpants, his attention was focused on my ass, and I absolutely loved it.

The locker room was empty, which wasn't unheard of this time of day. It's why I chose to come late-morning: fewer distractions and interruptions during my video. Less background noise. I found an empty locker and shoved my bag inside, then I sat on the narrow wooden bench and began to untie my shoes. The door to a bathroom stall banged against the tile wall, and the sound echoed throughout the empty room. Apparently, I wasn't completely alone. Just as I bent over to remove my sneaker, I was grabbed roughly by my shoulders, my body hauled up against a solid chest at my back. Shock temporarily robbed my voice. Then an arm leveraged across my throat. The voice of the person assaulting me hissed in my ear like a snake, making my body shiver with revulsion.

"Don't move. Don't say one word." His lips brushed the shell of my ear, and I shook my head hard to push him away. "I imagined our first meeting being in a nicer place than this, but you're a hard man to track down. Never alone. Always with that jackass who follows you everywhere like a lost puppy."

I knew instantly who was holding me hostage. Steven fucking Masters. The shiny steel switchblade in his hand gleamed under the fluorescent lighting. One wrong move, and it would cut through the skin of my neck.

I swallowed, feeling the knife pressing to my skin as my throat expanded. "Someone could walk in any minute. And that jackass is standing right outside the door. If I scream, he will come running."

He tightened the tip of the knife against my throat, nicking the skin. It stung like a bad paper cut, and I wondered if I was bleeding.

"Then don't fucking scream."

He bit the shell of my ear, and it was all I could do not to headbutt him, but the knife threatened to slit my Adam's apple if I dared move just half an inch. Anger rushed through me, hot and swift. I was mad that I let myself be caught off guard. Infuriated that this man thought he had the right to put his lips on any part of my body or threaten me with a weapon. Exhausted from constantly looking over my shoulder and running. There was no room for fear with this much fury roiling through my blood. It made me act instinctively and impulsively.

My heart beat triple time. The whooshing of blood rushing through my ears was loud enough to drown out all other noises as I stood and bent forward, bringing him with me. With his arm still wrapped around my throat, and his other wrapped around my midsection, he followed the momentum of my body. Steven Masters hit the tiled floor headfirst with a sickening crunch. The force of his body toppling over mine brought me down with him, and I planted my knee into his stomach, knocking the wind from him. His head rolled listlessly to the side and his hand slackened, releasing his grip on the knife. It fell to the floor with a clatter, and I grabbed it and held it at the ready, just in case he regained consciousness.

I seethed with anger, my breath coming fast and short, rapid pants mixed with a spray of saliva. My face felt hot, and my neck burned. I touched my fingers to the cut and realized my skin was wet with blood. It coated my hand in a crimson stain. He must have cut me again when I stood.

"Graham! Help! Someone... Anyone... help me!"

I screamed at the top of my lungs until my voice became hoarse on the last words. The door to the locker room banged open, reverberating against the wall, and two men rushed in. One of them was Graham.

"Fuck!" He ran to me and kneeled by my side, grabbing the knife from my hand. "You're bleeding."

I could only nod. Graham eased me off Steven's body, and I sat back on my ass with a thud. I must have been in shock because I couldn't seem to find my voice. It was like watching a movie unfold before my eyes. I heard Graham and the other man talking, but it sounded so far away, like background noise. The beating of my heart sounded much louder, drowning out their voices. My neck burned, and I closed my eyes and tipped my head back to rest against the wooden bench at my back.

I drifted away, losing track of time. I didn't need to pay attention. Didn't need to remain alert. Graham was here, and I was safe. He would take care of everything. Even with my eyes closed, I could see. The emerald green of the pine trees that swayed in the breeze. The crystal blue water of the swimming hole. The rushing water capped with white foam in the creek behind Graham's cabin. And I could hear. The songbirds in the trees. The creaking of the old wooden rocking chair on the porch.

It was the most unlikely place a guy like me would call home.

It was my salvation.

"Open your eyes and sit up for me. Kelley. Come on, sit up and open your eyes."

No! My mind screamed. I didn't want to open my eyes because then I couldn't see. I would lose sight of the only place I could think of that would comfort me right now. I felt his hands slide behind my back, urging me to sit up, his thumb stroking my jaw softly. His deep smooth voice in my ear, giving me an anchor to the present. Something solid to hold on to. I blinked my eyes open and squinted as I stared up into the harsh fluorescent light. Those strong fingers gripped my chin and tilted my head down until I was staring into the greenest eyes, so full of concern—for me—and I leaned into his embrace, laying my head against his shoulder, chest to chest.

It seemed there were two places that could comfort me. And they were both tied to this man.

"He's gone, Fancy."

I looked over his shoulder to see the paramedics carrying Steven Masters out on a stretcher. Another team hovered behind Graham, watching me.

"These people want to check you out." I shook my head. I couldn't bear to leave his strong, safe arms. "No, let them. I need to know that you're okay. Please, Kelley."

For him, I would do anything. Even bear the touch of a stranger right now, so soon after Steven Masters had touched me. Violated me. I could still feel his breath on my ear, his tongue, wet and hot. My stomach recoiled with nausea, and I swallowed down the bile that rose in my throat. It burned a sour trail down to the pit of my stomach. Graham scooted back as the team moved in to take his place beside me on the floor, and I reached out to him. He took hold of my hand, squeezing so tightly.

"Don't let go."

"Never. I've got you."

Always.

I sat still like a good boy while the EMTs checked me out. I didn't even feel the pain anymore. The warm, solid weight of Graham's hand in mine, squeezing reassuringly, was the only thing I could feel. My eyes remained locked on him, never wavering throughout the check up.

"Looks like four butterfly bandages will do the trick. It's not deep enough to need stitches," the EMT assessed.

Graham exhaled with relief. "We're just waiting for Detective Vallejo. She wants to talk with you before I take you home."

His rough fingers stroked my cheek, his touch as tender as the look in his eyes, and I lost myself in the sensation of his warm calloused skin against the smoothness of mine.

The detective arrived ten minutes later and took a

seat on the bench beside me. It took twenty more minutes to recount what happened and answer her questions.

"It's over Kelley. You did so good. I doubt he'll be granted bail. He's going to serve time for this. And you won't have to worry about looking over your shoulder anymore."

For some reason, her words didn't give me the satisfaction I imagined they would.

"What is it, sweetheart?" Graham's hand stroked down my spine.

"I'd rather he get the help he needs than just be punished." Detective Vallejo's surprised brown eyes glanced at Graham questioningly before settling back on me.

"I can certainly recommend that to the judge. Or the DAs office, if they settle out of court. Let me know if you change your mind."

And then, I was buckled into Graham's truck, and he carried me away from the scene where months of constant stalking and stress had finally come to an end.

"Kelley, what are you feeling?"

I shook my head, glancing from the window to his face. "I don't know. I guess it just doesn't really feel finished. Like it's anticlimactic. I expected explosions and a car chase. I've built it up in my mind for so long now, I just can't believe it's over."

Graham chuckled, the sound a warm deep rumble rolling through his chest. "Thank God it wasn't. The man held a knife to your throat. How much more climax do you need?"

When we arrived home, I paused in the foyer and

looked around. It felt as if it had been ten years since I last stood here, instead of just hours.

Graham's strong hand landed on my back, between my shoulder blades. "Why don't you go get in bed? I'll join you in a minute."

Despite the sun shining through the patio doors, getting into bed sounded lovely, and very necessary. I just wanted to hide under the covers and shut the world away while I processed everything that had happened and how I felt about it.

Woodenly, I walked through the house, through the living room, and into our bedroom, where I removed my clothes, now tainted with Steven's touch, and let them pool on the floor in a discarded pile before climbing between the cool sheets. More than anything, I wanted to take a shower, to let the scalding hot water cleanse my skin of his touch, but I just didn't have the energy to stand upright that long. The crash of adrenaline had robbed me of strength.

When I was settled, I heard Graham moving around the house, locking doors, setting the alarm, and tinkering in the kitchen. Finally, he shuffled into the bedroom and drew the curtains closed, shutting out the chaotic world beyond. I was cocooned in darkness, and it felt...safe. Graham appeared at the side of the bed, holding a fluffy white ball of fur.

"I think somebody wants to cuddle with you."

He peeled the covers down from my chin so Glitter could crawl inside my makeshift cave. She snuggled in the crook of my neck, swiping my face with her fluffy tail. Her tiny little body purred like a powerful engine, and I soaked up the vibration and let it scatter my heavy thoughts as I smiled and squeezed her a little tighter to me. Kitten cuddles were exactly what I needed. I was only missing one thing. And a moment later, he crawled under the covers and joined me, snuggling up to my back and wrapping his arms around my waist to spoon me in his embrace. I had everything I needed right here in this bed. Everything that mattered, that I loved, was either cuddled up to me or holding onto me, as if I were the most important person in the world.

I FELT WEIGHTLESS. Warm and light. Like I could just jump into the air, and with the tiniest boost, my body could fly away. A rough, wet tongue licked insistently at my lips, coaxing me to open them.

"Mmm, good morning."

The deep, rumbly voice purred in my ear. I wanted more of that, more of that demanding mouth on mine, and I parted my lips to welcome his tongue inside.

"Ugh!"

I spit out a mouthful of hair and swiped my hand over my lips. When I opened my eyes, I stared right into the fluffy white face of the prettiest kitten, who was looking at me with big green, innocent eyes. Heedless of my theatrics, she crept closer and began to lick my face again. Graham chuckled, the sound of his laughter felt like a warm blanket over my body.

"Tell me you didn't think it was me. I promise you, I'm a better kisser than Glitter."

With a smile on my lips, I pushed back against his body, burrowing into his solid warmth. "She's a wonderful kisser, I just wasn't expecting a mouth full of fur," I defended.

Graham's soft lips pressed against my cheek, and I had to admit, it felt even better than Glitter's kiss. I turned my face up to meet his. His beautiful green eyes were full of concern.

"How do you feel today? Be warned, I'm not letting you out of this bed until you tell me you feel a hundred percent. You slept all of yesterday and through the night." I started to panic but he calmed me by placing his hand on my chest. "Don't worry, I took care of Glitter."

"In that case, I feel awful. Completely horrible." I grinned, hoping to convince him to stay in bed with me all day.

His skeptical look said he wasn't buying that. He brushed his fingers through my hair. "I worry about you. You cover a lot of pain with a pretty smile. Don't hide from me."

I swallowed and breathed in a deep, steadying breath. "I'm okay. Not fantastic, but not a cause for concern either. I just need time to process everything that's happened and make peace with it so I can let it go. I have so many different thoughts and feelings competing for top spot in my head and my heart, and I just need time to sort it all out."

Graham let go of my waist, and his big body shifted like he was going to roll away from me. I gripped his thick forearm, holding him in place. "I need time, not space. Don't go anywhere. I need you just like this."

To prove my point, I pushed my bottom against his erection, and he pushed back, nestling his bare cock between my cheeks.

"What kinds of thoughts and feelings?"

I closed my eyes as I spoke, pretending that it made me safer. "Overanalyzing my reactions. Wondering if there was something I could've done differently."

Graham's strong fingers cupped my chin and angled my face toward him, and I opened my eyes and met his direct green stare.

"Kelley, there was nothing you could have done differently that would have made a better outcome, for him or you. His actions are not your responsibility. You were a victim of his behavior and his choices. Do not carry the burden of his guilt."

He brushed his lips softly over mine, the barest caress of his mouth, like an intimate hug.

"You're right. I know you're right, in my head. But my heart is so mixed up. I know you'll think I'm crazy for saying this, but I actually feel bad for him, and at the same time, I hate him for scaring me, for forcing me to change my life and my routine, even if it brought me closer to you."

"Those are all perfectly normal feelings. There's nothing wrong with you for being compassionate toward him, and yet, angry on your own behalf."

Unexpectedly, my chest grew heavy, and tears gathered in my eyes. "You are my rock. Steady and strong. That's the other thing I'm feeling."

"What?" His thumb stroked over my cheek to swipe a

tear that escaped. "What are you feeling?" His voice was soft as honey.

"All this love for you. Yesterday I realized that he could have hurt you instead of me. The thought scared the shit out of me. I felt so angry, even though it hadn't happened, and that's when I realized..."

"Realized what?"

"That I'm in love with you. That you're the most important thing in the world to me," I said, as I covered Glitter's ears with my hands. I couldn't let her think she wasn't my number one priority. What kind of cat dad would that make me?

Ignoring Glitter's mewling protests, Graham maneuvered my body so I was flush against his, chest to chest, hips to hips, our legs tangled in a knot with no beginning, and no end. With a withering glare, she flicked her fluffy tail and jumped to the floor.

"I love you, too. I know this is new, but I'm sure about us. I'm sure of my feelings. They are only going to grow stronger every day, every year."

My face was buried in the crook of his neck, but I raised my head to look into his face. "You love me?" I could see it in his smile, in his eyes.

"I love you. I'm crazy about you. I love your kind soul, your huge generous heart, your flair and vivaciousness, your zest for life, and your endless capacity to love and forgive. Plus, you're a great cook and you look great in lingerie." He said with a wink.

I exhaled a breath full of relief and contentment. "I'm completely, totally, head over heels about you, and you're absolutely right, it's only going to get worse from here. Prepare yourself," I teased with a mischievous smile.

"I'm totally prepared. I can't wait."

He pressed his lips to mine and slid his tongue inside my mouth, brushing and rubbing against my own until I was completely convinced of his feelings for me.

When he pulled away to take a breath, I asked, "Would you do something for me?"

"Anything. I would do anything for you."

"Take me away from here. Take me to our special place where time doesn't exist. Where there's no work and commitments. No phone calls or visitors. Take me to Rook Mountain."

EPILOGUE
GRAHAM

AS WE GOT CLOSER, I rolled down the windows to breathe in the fresh air. The pine-scented breeze never failed to release something in my chest, an invisible weight of accumulated daily stressors, and now a stalker who had threatened the man I love, as well. Inhaling through my nose, I held it in my lungs until I felt lighter, and then released the burdened breath.

When I glanced over at my passenger, I couldn't hide my smile. Dressed in a red and white checked blouse and white capri pants, Kelley looked like a picnic tablecloth. He had removed his large white sunglasses and had his head tipped back against the seat's headrest. Bright sunlight bathed his face, highlighting the chiseled angles of his high cheekbones and square jaw. He wore a soft contented smile on his painted-red lips as he cuddled his kitten in his lap.

I chuckled. Glitter was watching me, her fluffy tail swishing lazily against Kelley's chest. She was dressed in a matching checked shirt, and when she began to knead her tiny paws on Kelley's thigh, I noticed he had painted her razor-thin claws bright red, to match his own.

What a pair they made.

Adorable and refreshing.

Charming.

Mine.

The miles flew by one by one in a blissful relaxed silence, and before long, I was pulling the truck off the highway and turning onto the access road that wound up Rook Mountain. Kelley opened his eyes and sat up.

"We're here!"

I could hear the excitement in his voice as he explained the rules to Glitter.

"You need to be a good kitty. No running off chasing after squirrels. No hiding from Daddy and Papa in the nooks and crannies of the cabin. I brought your cat bed, your tree, and your scratching post, and you can thank me by not getting lost. Or dirty," he added with a wrinkle of his cute nose.

Who would have ever thought I'd have a little family of my own to look after? Certainly not me. *Fuck*, I was so damn lucky.

It took longer than expected to move all of Glitter's paraphernalia from the bed of my truck into the house. It was like traveling with a real baby. There was even a stroller! Kelley had been worried about putting Glitter on the leash up here, that she might step on a burr or thorn, so he had ordered a stroller that had an enclosed mesh and plastic carrier where the seat would normally go. It was official! I was a cat dad. And by that, I meant I'd officially lost my mind over a cat and her daddy.

Which made Kelley a DILF. I laughed to myself as I grabbed Glitter's cat condo from the truck bed and flipped the tailgate up. It was amazing how much my life had changed, and for the better, since they had come into it and flipped all the shades open, letting the sunshine pour inside.

I trailed behind Kelley as he stopped to point out each colorful flower along the stone path that led up to the cabin. He spoke to his cat as if she understood every word. And she gave him her undivided attention in return, licking at his nose.

And that's when it hit me.

The decision that would change the rest of my life.

I saw myself married to him. Trailing behind him ten years from now, twenty years, as we carried our fur family into the cabin. Returning to celebrate holidays, anniversaries, and birthdays, *together*.

I wanted it. More than my next breath. More than I'd ever wanted anything. And I knew exactly how to get it.

As soon as I finished unpacking our stuff, I would put my plan into motion.

I GRABBED my keys from the counter and kissed Kelley's cheek. "I'll be back soon. Running out to get groceries."

"Oh! Can you pick up lemonade?"

"You're at the cabin now, Fancy. We make our lemonade fresh here." I winked, and he swatted my ass, laughing.

"In that case, can you pick up some lemons?"

"You bet."

I hurried to my truck and down the mountain, eager to get going. My first stop was the huge antique mall. I was able to find what I needed fairly quickly. The second item on my list involved a little more patience and searching. Eventually, after more than an hour of browsing aisle after dusty aisle, my eyes landed on the perfect choice. In a jeweler's case full of antique estate jewelry, behind a wall of scratched and chipped glass, the ring sparkled like it had been set just yesterday, instead of decades ago. The emeralds and sapphires shone under the fluorescent lighting like colorful fire. I thought they represented the colors of our eyes perfectly. The center stone was a princess cut diamond, fit for a princess like mine, and flanked by the rich baguette gems on all sides. The stones were set in platinum that shined beautifully.

"Can I see that one?" I tapped the glass to point to the one I had my eye on. The vendor unlocked the case and handed it to me.

It was gorgeous. Flawless, like Kelley. When I tilted it to inspect the band for scratches, I noticed an engraving inside.

Eternally mine. Forever yours.

It was absolutely perfect. "I'll take it."

He packaged it up, and I headed for my second stop, the general store, for groceries. As I shopped for the things I thought we'd need, my phone beeped, alerting me to an incoming text. I pulled out my phone and read the message from Shannon. It was basically a long laundry list of complaints about his cousin Gordy. There was some sort of disagreement in the kitchen, at the lounge, which led to a disagreement behind the bar, which led to a disagreement in the store room about supplies, which led to a physical tussle that my nephew Carson had to split up. I put the phone back in my pocket, deciding to ignore the message for now. I was focused on Kelley, not the boys. I would never understand the hostility between my son and my nephew. They used to be so close. Almost like brothers. Hell, there was a time when I thought it would turn into more. To see what they had become was heartbreaking.

By the time I parked back at the cabin, Kelley had finished unpacking and was lounging in the sun on a blanket in the grass. I hurried inside to stash my present and drop off the food before joining him outside. Kneeling on the blanket, I crowded over his body, blocking out the sun's rays, and brushed my lips over his.

"Hey, beautiful. Feeling relaxed?"

"Mmm. I needed this so bad."

"What else do you need?" My voice sounded husky with need.

His heated gaze traveled down my body to where my dick, hard and thick, pressed between his legs. "An even tan."

"Huh?" That wasn't the answer I was anticipating.

Kelley chuckled and began to unbutton his blouse. "No tan lines. No clothes."

My balls burned with my unspent load. I watched as he slid the cotton from his shoulders, his smooth bronzed skin gleaming in the sunshine. I spread my hands across his chest, grazing his tight nipples. He squirmed and shimmied his pants down his legs. My breath caught as he lay between my thighs wearing nothing but red lace panties. No doubt, he'd chosen them to match the shirt he wore, which made me smile. My fingers itched to touch him, to explore him.

"You're so beautiful."

His lips parted on a breathy sigh. "Show me."

I whipped my T-shirt off quickly, tossing it aside, and reached for the button on my jeans. I made a mess of getting them off, falling on my ass as I worked them down my legs. Impatience made me sloppy, but who could blame me? He was hot as fuck with his red lips, red nails stroking the hard length concealed by red lace. I had to touch him, taste him, right now. When I was stripped bare, I kneeled over him again and dipped down to claim his lips as my cock brushed against his.

"Where's the cat?"

"Napping inside," he breathed, breathless with desire.

I sat back on my knees and slid my hands under his thighs, lifting him to meet me. I lined up my dick between his cheeks, catching the wet head of my cock on the lace that covered the crease between his cheeks. The friction felt amazing.

"Push it in," Kelley urged. I couldn't, not with his panties between us, but the idea made me hard as hell.

I grazed my cockhead against his sac, rubbing back and forth until he begged. "Please, Graham. Use me."

Christ! He always knew exactly what to say to make me desperate for him.

He reached for the elastic band to push them down

his legs. "Leave them on. I want to watch the lace rub against your cock as I fuck you."

"Oh God. Do it," he whined.

I held him with one arm and slid the fingers of my other hand between his lips. "Suck them."

His scarlet lips pulled sweetly on my fingers. With his cheeks hollowed out, he looked absolutely filthy. I withdrew them and a line of his saliva remained, connecting them to his mouth. His tongue peeked out to catch it, and I groaned.

"Damn, baby. That mouth of yours is sinful."

Sliding his panties aside, I slid my fingers between his cheeks, rubbing over his tight hole. His puckered skin felt smooth and warm, and I snuck a long thick finger past his entrance. His muscles squeezed me deliciously, and I imagined how good it would feel around my cock. I added another finger, stroking in and out of him slowly, searching out his P spot. With his lower half still suspended midair, his crotch snugged up to mine, he began to hump against my dick in sync with my finger fucking.

"That's it, baby. Ride me. Chase that feeling."

With his head tipped back, eyes closed, lips parted, he looked wanton and debauched. The sunlight filtered through the leaves of the tree, casting a dappled shadow on his face. He looked beautiful. His fists clutched the blanket desperately as he writhed against my body.

"Touch my dick. Please."

How could I say no when he asked so nicely?

I lowered my mouth and sucked him through the thin

lace, licking down his length. The panties barely contained his erection, the wet shiny head peeking out the top of the waistband. It leaked copiously, leaving a milky puddle on his smooth toned stomach. I reached up to lick him clean, and he gasped, eyes flying open to watch as my tongue stroked over his sensitive skin. I continued to tunnel my finger into his channel, and Kelley's mouth opened around a silent scream. I saw his orgasm in his face, eyes going wide, before his seed rushed from his cock in a hot mess.

I pulled his panties down to bunch up under his balls and fitted my aching cock against his. Using his cum as lube, I stroked our cocks together in my fist, stroking and squeezing until I shouted as my release landed on his stomach. It sprayed in thick white ropes and spurts across his tanned skin, and I reached forward to lick it off.

"Give me your tongue," he begged.

My lips moved over his as I shared my flavor with him, and Kelley moaned into my mouth.

Yeah, sign me up for a fucking lifetime of this. With him.

WE ATE a simple dinner of grilled chicken breast over salad on the front porch as we watched the sun set over the mountain. We were so high up in elevation, it felt as if we could reach out and touch the setting sun from here. Kelley laid his head against my shoulder as he chewed, and the smell of his body spray wafted up into my face. Lemon verbena. If I had to place bets, I'd say it was purposeful, to compliment the freshly-squeezed lemonade he'd served with dinner.

My Fancy didn't do anything half-assed, he went all out. Always. I loved that about him. His flair for life, his obsession with patterning himself after a sitcom housewife. Partly, it was his natural personality to just be fabulous. But I suspected a part of it had to do with working toward perfection in the misguided hope it would fix what his family couldn't accept about him. He was searching for happiness and love. The perfect family. The perfect life.

Weren't we all?

I hoped that picture looked a little different for him now since he'd met me. That I'd shown him he could relax a little, show his imperfections, and still be loved and accepted.

He sighed. "Wouldn't it be lovely if we could stay here forever?"

"If you want, we can make it work."

"Really?" Kelley sat up, looking surprised.

"Sure. Whatever would make you happy."

"Nah," he said, laughing. "There's no mall!"

"There's an antique mall. Does that count?" I asked, knowing it didn't.

"Not even close. Take me back to the city," he teased.

I pressed a kiss on his head, inhaling his citrusy scent. "I love you, Fancy." The words were spoken softly, on a breath.

He set his salad bowl down by his feet and burrowed his head into my chest. "I love you, Graham," he said in a sigh as he looked out over the orange horizon.

I squeezed him tighter. Tonight. I would ask him tonight.

SATED from our earlier lovemaking in the sun, we spent the night cuddled together on the old worn sofa, underneath one of my mama's handmade blankets, watching an old Bruce Willis classic on my ancient VHS player. Kelley wore pink satin pjs: short shorts and a button-up short-sleeved top with white kittens on them that looked suspiciously like Glitter. On his feet, he wore fluffy white cat slippers. With every step he took, Glitter viciously attacked the cats, swiping her dagger-like claws at them in a bid for dominance. It was hilarious, so much so that I volunteered Kelley to get up and refill our popcorn bowl, just so I could laugh as I watched him try to dart to the kitchen ahead of the ninja kitten.

"He reminds me of you," he said when he was settled by my side again.

"Bruce? Tell me I'm not that bald, please."

Kelley laughed. "No, not the hair. The confidence and swagger. The muscles. The hot Zaddyness. The white-knight complex, always playing the hero, like you did for me." He sighed, smiling. "You could star in an action movie," he said, squeezing my biceps. I flexed the muscles, enjoying the attention.

"I doubt it. But we could certainly make our own action movie," I suggested, wiggling my brows.

"We could," he agreed with a flirty smile. "On that note, I'm going to go and shower."

He trampled over the cat as he raced to the bedroom, trying his best to outpace her without tripping over her. I jumped to my feet and cleaned up the living room and kitchen before going straight for the bedroom. I had only minutes to set up my surprise while he showered. Opening the drawer of my nightstand where I'd stashed everything from his curious eyes, I removed the squat mason jar candles and lit them, placing them around the room. Next, I set my gift upon the dresser, the one he kept his clothes in. I didn't know what to do with myself as I waited, where to stand. My hands fidgeted nervously, and I realized I was pacing in tight circles. Finally, I sat down on the edge of the bed, tucking my hands beneath my legs to keep them still. When I heard the water shut off, my heart began to pound painfully hard in my chest.

Fuck. What if he said no? What if he laughed?

That's not Kelley. That's not the man you fell in love with, I reminded myself.

Another fifteen minutes passed, and I imagined he was applying lotion and other mysterious serums to his flawless skin. Then the door opened, and he trailed out wrapped in a towel, his smooth skin deliciously pink and damp. Kelley stood before the dresser and opened the top drawer, selecting a clean pair of purple panties and a matching satin pajama set. He shut the drawer and bent to slip the panties over his feet, dropping his towel and pulling them up his long toned legs. When he straightened, he paused, his eyes finally landing on the strange box that seemingly had appeared out of nowhere. Kelley touched the enameled box, running his fingers lovingly over the inlaid surface.

"Where did this come from? It's lovely."

"Open it," I rasped, then cleared my throat.

He looked at me curiously before returning to the box. Kelley opened the lid and a tiny ballerina popped up, made of plastic and wearing a pink tutu. She turned in a graceful swirl on her toes, around and around. The music sounded tinny and off key, revealing its age. I was not prepared for the tears that shimmered in his beautiful eyes when he turned around.

"I've always dreamed of having a music box like this when I was little. I saw one at the department store and asked my mom for it." He shook his head. "Of course, she said it was for girls, and that I couldn't have it."

It was hard to swallow past the emotions thickening my throat. I had no idea when I chose it that it meant something to him. I just thought it made pretty packaging. It also reminded me of him, a graceful dancer, so beautiful and poised.

"It's yours," I choked out.

"What's this?" He lifted the small midnight blue velvet box from within. "Did it belong to your mother?"

"No, baby. That's for you, too."

His pretty eyes widened in shock, and he swiped the tears that rolled down his cheeks. "For me?"

I wondered when was the last time he'd been given a special gift like this? Maybe never?

"Open it."

He nodded, a teary strangled laugh escaping from his mouth. "Good Lord, let me put some clothes on first."

As he turned his back to me to slip into his pajamas, I got down on my knee behind him. When he turned around, he gasped, his manicured hand flying up to cover his mouth.

"Open it," I repeated.

He swallowed, reached for the box atop the dresser, and lifted the lid.

"Graham, oh God."

His hand shook as he lifted the ring from its velvet nest. Gently, I took it from him and held it up, like an offering, as I took his hand in mine to steady it.

"I've never found anything that shines brighter than you do, not even this ring. But I might, if you agree to wear it." I watched his throat bob as he struggled to hold back his emotions. "Kelley Michaelson, will you marry me? I want to spend the rest of my life loving you, spoiling you—and Glitter. Please say yes."

"Yes! Oh my God, yes!" He wrapped his arms around my neck so tightly I coughed. And fuck if my eyes weren't also growing wet. In that one word, he'd given me everything.

Yes to a lifetime of creating unforgettable memories.

Yes to decades of love and laughter.

Yes to creating our own family and sharing my family with him.

Yes to having a hand to hold through every dark day in my future.

Yes to becoming my husband.

"Graham?" He lifted his head and raised his eyes to mine. "Can I take your last name?"

I couldn't answer, couldn't speak. I crushed him to me, letting the ridiculous tears roll down my cheeks into my beard.

Kelley Carrick. *Fucking perfect.*

I let him go, cleared my throat, and slipped the ring on his finger.

"You are definitely a Carrick, Fancy. Through and through. Forever. You're home now, with us, with *me*. You can take my last name and everything that goes with it. Just promise you'll love me forever."

He kissed me, a little too hard, a little too quickly. "I already do."

START FROM THE BEGINNING

Want to start from the beginning? Download **Mimosas And Mixers**, the prequel to the *Love And Libations* series.

Are you ever too old to fall in love? What are the odds you'll end up with the first boy you ever crushed on?

Nate

Running into Charlie at our high school reunion was kismet. I can't imagine myself with anyone else. Is it too late for a second chance at love?

Charlie

Nate is everything I dreamt of finding in a partner. Except, he's my son's therapist. Will their professional relationship come between our personal one? Or does fate have other plans for us?

Mimosas and Mixers is the prequel to the Love and Libations series. This sweet heat gay romance novella includes cameos from the Hearts For Hire Series and features tropes such as second chances, a mature couple, childhood friends, and found family.

ALSO BY RAQUEL RILEY

Want to catch up with the Hearts For Hire series? Start from the beginning with Lucky Match and work your way through all of the escorts' happily ever afters!

After one date, I realized that would never be enough...

Lucky Maguire

I started Lucky Match, a dating service, as an enjoyable way to earn some extra cash. That's how I ended up on a date with my super hot Economics Professor.

Here's my three step plan to seduce my teacher:

Convince Hayes to fake date me.

Inform him that we were never fake dating; it was always real.

Make him fall in love with me.

How many dates will it take for Hayes to realize I'm his lucky match?

Hayes Brantley

After my divorce, I decided it's time for a change. After missing being with a man for the past twelve years of my loveless marriage, I'm finally free to make up for lost time.

I called Lucky Match to hookup with someone who looks like the sexy student I can't stop fantasizing about. I had no idea I'd end up with the real deal.

Is a second chance at love worth risking my career and another broken heart?

ABOUT THE AUTHOR

Raquel Riley is a native of South Florida but now calls North Carolina home. She is an avid reader and loves to travel. Most often, she writes gay romance stories with an HEA but characters of all types can be found in her books. She weaves pieces of herself, her family, and her travels into every story she writes.

For a complete list of Raquel Riley's releases, please visit her website at **www.raquelriley.com**. You can also follow her on the social media platforms listed below. You can also find all of Raquel's important links in one convenient place at **https://linktr.ee/raquelriley**

ACKNOWLEDGMENTS

A huge thank you to **Tracy Ann**. Your invaluable feedback and dedication to my boys makes all the difference in my books. You are an angel without wings.

Finn Dixon, without your help and considerable talent, this book would have been forever a first draft. I'll never find the right words to tell you how much I appreciate you.

Odessa Hywell, thank you for always answering when I call with endless questions, or just to spitball. You keep me sane. Also, You made the most beautiful covers for this series!

Dianna Roman, Why aren't you sick of me yet? Thank you for your continued praise and support of my books.

To the **86'rs,** You ladies make me laugh every day, encourage me to write absolute filth, and convince me that people want to read it. You are the best group of friends a gal could wish for.

Also, thank you to my **ARC/street team** for your insightful input and reviews.

Last, but never least, thanks to my family for being so understanding while I ignore you so I can write.